Sidelined with a dislocated shoulder, shortstop Zan Hagen can only watch, frustrated, as the Robert E. Lee Generals play.

Walking home, I felt angry and useless. I hadn't helped my team for almost a week. Who knows when I might be able to boom again. Even Rinehart couldn't promise me. He had no schemes right then for wrecked human bodies. Not saying a word, he puffed along beside me, swinging his log in his left hand and his briefcase with a healthy right arm. What's he doing with that arm, I wondered. He can't catch. He can't hit. Sadder than ever, I held my own left arm against my right one. I put on some speed to sluff off my pal. I ran ahead of him. I gave up more.

From way down the street he called, "You still have your legs."

R. R. KNUDSON was born in Washington, D.C., and grew up in Arlington, Virginia. She received a B.A. from Brigham Young University, an M.A. from the University of Georgia, and a Ph.D. from Stanford. In addition to the other Zan Hagen books (*Zanballer* and *Zanbanger*), Knudson is the author of the action-packed *Jesus Song* and *You Are the Rain* and a volume of poetry, *Sports Poems* (all available in Laurel-Leaf editions).

LAUREL-LEAF BOOKS bring together under a single imprint outstanding works of fiction and nonfiction particularly suitable for young adult readers both in and out of the classroom. The series is under the editorship of Charles F. Reasoner, Professor of Elementary Education, New York University.

ALSO AVAILABLE IN LAUREL-LEAF BOOKS:

ZANBOOMER

by R. R. Knudson

LAUREL-LEAF
BOOKS

Published by
Dell Publishing Co., Inc.
1 Dag Hammarskjold Plaza
New York, New York 10017

Laurel-Leaf Library ® TM 766734, Dell Publishing Co., Inc.

ISBN: 0-440-99908-1

Reprinted by arrangement with Harper & Row, Publishers, Inc.

Printed in the United States of America

First Laurel-Leaf printing—August 1980

For Johnnee Matthews Cunningham,
who runs to a different drummer

ZANBOOMER

Chapter 1

Click.

Click.

Click.

My spikes took our dugout steps one at a time, careful not to slip on damp concrete. No point breaking a leg the first day of practice.

Clickity, clickity, clickity.

New season, new shoes—nickel spikes and white kid leather. Best pair in the Wilson sports catalog.

Clickity click. Clickity click.

Over to the water cooler. Coach O'Hara had printed DO NOT GULP on a piece of tape and stuck it near a dispenser of paper cups. I sipped, watching across the soggy diamond for our team. I was early because Rinehart had forged me an excuse from my seventh-period study hall: "Kindly allow my daughter, Suzanne Hagen, to consult with her physician about various medical complications requiring periodic attention during baseball season. Very truly yours, James Hagen."

"With this note you'll escape study hall any day you want," Rinehart had vowed, signing my father's name with a flourish. He added the date: Monday, March 27.

"Every day is perfect," I told him. "Rinehart, you could skip and come with me if only you knew how to throw a ball so it gets there—anywhere. Or if you knew how to catch with a hand, not a shin. Or hit. Bunt or that."

"I can forge. See you after practice, Zan" is all Rinehart answered.

He can forge for sure. Write exactly the same as anyone's father. Plus get A's in every subject, most of all math and science. Arthur Rinehart, winner of three science fairs in a row since he came to Robert E. Lee Junior-Senior High. Publisher of *Rinehart's Science Newsletter* right in his own basement laboratory. Down there he collects gerbils and vampire bats, not baseballs and slugging bats. He studies butterflies while I chase fly balls. We're total opposites— alter egos, he always says. After that he says another scientific theory: "Opposites attract." I wished he were here in the dugout right now with his dissecting knife to nip off this fringy leather on my infielder's glove.

Where is everybody? Where's our team?

I made a fist and socked my glove pocket while I paced in front of the bench. Click. Sock. Click. Sock. My shoes spattered mud I'd brought from the swampy bull pen. Spring rains in Virginia don't help your fielding average any. The ball takes goofy hops. Errors botch up the team record book. Coach O'Hara counts errors during practice even in typhoon conditions. He'd soon be counting today. He'd be on field with his clipboard and whistle.

My glove warmed my hand. My tight-fitting cap warmed my head. Thoughts of the weeks ahead warmed me up in the face. I flushed with happiness.

2

First we'd practice until the nine of us could make any newspaper's All-Star Lineup. Then we'd play early-April exhibitions with teams not in our league, maybe with schools across the river in Washington. I hadn't seen our schedule. I hoped for D.C. Memorial and Herbert Hoover High. Their pitchers were patsies to tee off on. After fattening our batting averages, we'd play in the Class "A" Virginia High School League, Northern Division. We'd win and win. On our pitcher Randy Boyle's fastball. On Ben Brown's glove in center field. On DumDum Cadden's big bat. Before mid season we'd meet our most hated rivals, the Richmond Redskins of the Southern Division. POW. Our Fritz would kiss a triple to the fence. ZIP. Our Aileen would steal second base, third base, home. We'd win on power, teamwork, coaching—one of everything.

Ummm. No doubt we'd face Richmond again in June at the Virginia State Series. We'd beat them on a grand slammer by me maybe.

I was dreaming so hard I didn't hear our second baseman, Monk Cunningham, until his spikes hit the bottom step. He gave me a welcoming squeeze. I felt his St. Christopher medal grind into my chin. "Just don't crush my throwing arm, teammate," I said through a mouthful of uniform.

Monk backed away for a drink. He sat down to straighten his socks. He rebuckled his belt. "Where's our guys?" he asked without looking up from cleaning mud off his spikes. "We can't win if we don't practice—practice more than every other team in this state." He fished a small can from his deep back pocket, dunked 3-in-One oil into his glove where it said GRIP-TIGHT POCKET, and spread the oil with his fingertips. "Winning's best," he said. "You better believe it. Best."

"Best. Lend me a squirt of oil."

We sat together like two old pros, pounding our gloves, tipping our caps this way and that to find better angles, sharpening our spikes so they clicked more when we stood up for another round of drinks.

"Winning's all that matters," Monk said after he gargled his sip.

"How can we lose?" I wasn't really asking. I meant "No way we can lose."

Monk started in on the ways. "If Ben doesn't learn to hit curves. He's afraid of them. If Dum-Dum doesn't remember how many bases there are and which one to throw to. If Randy shows off as usual on the mound. If the Eagles or Warriors or Redskins make Eugene mad enough to kick the columns of this dugout so hard the sparks fly. He broke his toe last year, remember?"

I did. From the newspapers, not because I'd been in the dugout. I didn't play baseball for the Robert E. Lee Generals then. I was a rookie today. Healthy all over. Aiming to win.

But Monk hadn't finished. "The tiniest injury can cramp your swing or hobble you on the base paths." He rubbed his left eye. "Last season during play-offs I caught an elbow in a rundown. I wrecked my eye my next ten at bats. My average fell off. In the series I bruised my thigh sliding. Hurt me something awful."

4

"No sweat—you played." I remembered from the Washington *Herald*.

While Monk massaged his old wounds and mumbled glumly about new ones, I watched E.J. and Eugene slithering across the outfield. Spikes don't work all that well in a lagoon. E.J.'s warm-up jacket hung casually around her shoulders. She had to carry her mitt high to keep off Eugene's splashes. He charged out in front, turned around, and waited up for her. He stuck his glove under his belt and helped tie her jacket sleeves in a loose knot over her collarbone. They ran on together, E.J. with her graceful, loping stride, Eugene with his jerky bursts.

"Hey, the whole rest of our infield," I shouted.

Shoes full of water, spikes silenced by tufts of grass, they sloshed the three steps down to us: E. J. Johnston, first basewoman; Eugene Matello, third baseman. They touched gloves with Monk Cunningham, second baseman, and Zan Hagen, shortstop. Then we four stormed the field, a straight line of defenders. We'd catch fast, throw hard, tear up the league. We'd win 'em all. Together.

"Great fun," called E.J., stretching toward my peg to first base. She'd had the wits to bring a baseball so we didn't need to wait for Buddy, our equipment manager.

Us infielders began warming that ball. We whipped it around the bags, person to person. E.J. to Eugene. Eugene to Monk at second. Monk back to E.J. Her to me covering third as Eugene pretended to charge a bunt.

"All the way."

5

"Be ready."

"Make it move."

"Yes. Yes. Yes."

"Attaboy, E.J."

"Look around. OOOOps, 'scuse me."

"Isn't this the pits?" I hollered when the ball dropped dead in a puddle.

"I've played in worse," Monk answered. "Pick it up—up. Show me your quick, Zan."

I shoveled him the ball at second, close enough to see his skin glistening under his cap bill. His face reddened and grew more intense as he speared the baseball and fired it over to first. Thwap. "I love the sound of leather hitting leather," he told us teammates.

"Almost as super as wood socking leather. Thwack. It's a homer. TH–WAC–K!" I made the sound into a three-syllable exclamation.

THWACK. THWACK. THWACK. This time the real sound.

Coach O'Hara stood at the plate, hammering grounders and pop flies as fast as Buddy handed him baseballs. Coach didn't flex his bat in between hits or tug his cap or stamp mud off his shoes. He didn't shout "Way to hustle" if Monk or Eugene made diving catches or "Attagirl" when we did. He never stepped out of the batter's box for a half hour. We caught, caught, caught, caught, and rolled back balls to Buddy, who wiped them off with a towel before forking them over to Coach, one at a time.

E.J. seemed unruffled by the explosion of balls in her direction. Slim and swift, she worked around first

6

base with the smooth moves of a big leaguer. Eight years of playing the same position at summer camp had taught her how to range deep for the long ball. How to charge the short one. How to dig the ball out of grass as if it were a bull's-eye throw to first. Her solemn green eyes followed the ball from Buddy's hand to Coach O'Hara's bat, right out to her mitt. THWACK. THWAP. E.J. had it.

"Waytogo," I called to her because Coach didn't.

On the other side of our infield Eugene hadn't broken a sweat yet. I could see his dry black hair and unshiny neck when I ran behind him to back up a pop fly. It isn't exactly Speed City around his canvas bag. His "hot corner" is hot because of Eugene's temper, not his slow hands and feet. Never mind. He's got guts when some big Redskin or Warrior comes sliding, spikes up, toward him. He stands his canvas and makes the tag with two big hands shoved out hard. But Eugene can't move fast at all.

"Bad luck," I called, meaning a screamer beyond Eugene's reach.

He turned away and kicked third.

Coach doesn't let his players mess around. With a THWACK he lifted a blooper directly above Eugene's bushy hair.

"Eugene!" I signaled him.

He glanced up. He stabbed, but the ball fell fair beside him.

"That's what tantrums do for you every time," Coach scolded with his strong lungs. He stroked the next ball to Monk instead. And the next. And a dozen.

Monk crouched low, resting his hands on his knees. Close to the ground. Close to his bag. To get a quick jump on the hit, he kept his weight forward, on the balls of his feet. With each stop of a grounder he brought up a handful of mud. He smothered the ball. Each fly ball he caught high so he'd be ready to throw for the double play.

Monk low, Monk high. Monk making catches at the belt buckle after a dash left or right. He held on to the ball with a glove of Elmer's glue. He kept his balance in pools of water. Anything hit up the middle didn't have a chance with Monk Cunningham at second. Just then he turned his back on the diamond and chased a fly to the outfield.

I covered his base—or at least I stepped on it to get a better view of Monk in action. I sort of flopped my hands and admired him making a tough chance seem simple. As he trotted back to his turf I gave out with a mighty whistle. I used my muddy fingers. E.J. called, "Great catch." Eugene bucked up and joined in our celebration by clapping his glove against his cap. It got to feeling like a party on field, especially when Buddy swung the ball bag around his head— pennant style. Coach laid down his bat.

For a rest? Wrong. To pick up another bat, longer and thinner it looked from my position. With no smile, and a gesture to send me deeper, Coach O'Hara announced, "Dozen more to short-stop. You—Cunningham—Johnston—Matello—take a drink of water."

Some party!

Buddy opened a box at his feet and withdrew a

8

wad of tissue paper. From this he unwrapped a new baseball. The others were sponges by now. I could see the fresh red stitches standing in ridges when Buddy flipped that ball to Coach. The clean white leather was a huge contrast to the muddy bat, which Coach wasted no time swinging in my direction.

Some gift!

His first hit rolled through my dumb legs. No excuse. Except maybe my hands were cold from the wait—"My hands weren't all there yet," as Monk would say. I shook my wrists to start the blood flowing. I went into my crouch. And straightened up, charging a dribbler directly at me. Hit number two seemed like a cinch, but somehow I booted it across the pitcher's mound. I was nervous.

Coach paused for me to find the ball, roll it in, and return to my position on the grass between third and second base. I fidgeted and drew deep breaths, then caught his line drive in the chest. Not with my glove. Just with my shirt, skin, and bone. The ball knocked me down. I lay there thinking, "Some shortstop!" All those chest-high fastballs I'd thrown myself off the garage door for years and years. All the ones my brother had thrown me in the driveway or hit to me in the street while he practiced for American Legion games. What good had a thousand catches a day, spring and summer long, done me now with Coach counting errors?

He suddenly stood above me asking, "Okay?" His iron eyes stared hard for an answer. He seemed to be watching for blood to spout or ribs to pierce the big blue GENERALS on my uniform. When I answered,

"Okay," he shot out a hand, pulled me up, and said, "Nine more. Don't miss again." He walked me to my position, instructing me. "Almost every ground ball that goes by a shortstop goes under her glove. Play closer to the ground. Bend your knees and back. Get your glove down. Put your eye on the ball, from that box Buddy holds until you have the ball in your glove. Your head must be over the ball as you field it, not turned away to keep from getting hit. Ball shyness has no place on my team."

"Yes sir, no sir," I promised.

"Buddy, new balls," ordered Coach.

They came off the bat at all different angles, speeds, heights. THWACK. THWACK. THWACK. THWACK. THWACK. I kept my glove low and trapped one in the webbing. I leaped high for a gloved-hand catch of a liner. I stopped a slow grounder with my bare hand. A short fly ball brought me into the mound. A high foul sent me up against the fence behind third.

"That's more like it, Zan," Rinehart said. He hung on the fence, poking his dissecting knife through a chain link. "Cut off that flappy lace around the thumb," he told me, aiming the sharp blade at my glove.

"Can't now. Don't distract me. How long have you been here?" I asked on the sprint infield.

Rinehart called, "Since I finished your English homework in study hall. Watchit. Watchit!"

Coach O'Hara had slapped number nine of his dozen soundly to my left. I sprang to get in front of the ball. I didn't back off to round it up. I cut straight across the ball's path—the shortest route. I made a giant hop off both feet. I blocked the ball and jumped up ready to throw to first base. E.J. was back on her bag, so I did. Might as well remind Coach about my arm, my strongest weapon as a baseballer.

Did Coach hear the extra-loud Thwap in E.J.'s mitt? No way, because right then he lofted a fly over my head. I took off, not the way an outfielder would, running with an eye over my shoulder And I didn't backpedal, either. Instead I picked a spot where the ball would most likely land, ran there, looked up, and—plunk in my glove. I'd practiced that kind of catch a thousand times on the street in front of my house. I'd practiced the next hit, too, a slow bouncer I rushed to the right with a crossover step. I reached—THWAP

Screams and waves came from the fence where girls collected, waiting for the late bus. Lurleen Dewey yelled, "She's our dream player," meaning me, I suppose, because E.J. was out of action, landscaping the mud pies around first base, and Aileen Dickerson hadn't shown up yet. Must be me Lurleen's cheering. I tipped my cap.

Not a word from Coach. He tossed number twelve above the plate and pushed me the trickiest hit yet, a ball that zigzagged among mud ruts, sputtered, nearly skipped my glove. Nearly. I *looked* that ball into the pocket. I concentrated. From the box of new balls right into my left hand.

For my catch Lurleen shrieked louder, and Ruby Jean Twilly called, "How do you do it?"

"Like you and your baton twirling. Same differ-

11

ence. I practice a lot. In front of a mirror." I meant it. In my mom's full-length mirror I'd studied my moves to find things wrong with my leap and pivot, my pickoff motions, my backhand stab and sidearm throw. I'd asked my brother hundreds of times: "How can I get better?" Now I'd ask Coach.

"Keep thinking all the time. Keep moving. Run faster." He left the plate and jogged behind second base to hit fly balls to his outfielders.

Girls leaned against the fence, beckoning their favorites. Randy stopped warming up in the bull pen to wave at Lurleen. Fritz removed his catcher's mask so he could see his fans better. Eugene sat down on third and posed for a picture. "It won't come out well. Too overcast this afternoon," Rinehart warned the tall, bearded guy aiming a camera—Ronald Mergler, Jr., of the Washington *Herald.* He'd been covering the Generals' teams all year for his paper. "I'll take you expert pictures tomorrow when the sun comes out," Rinehart said. "Here, I'll give you a perfect story today."

He flipped pages in the notebook he always carries: Rinehart's Log. He handed his log over to Mr. Mergler, all the time explaining about us Generals. About our power hitting and sensational pitching. About our base running, best in the Northern Division last year and better this spring with Aileen and E.J. added to the lineup. Rinehart didn't mention me. He knew I'd rather throw and hit than run any day. But he mentioned me next, as part of the Generals' "magnificent infield, Lee's proudest possession."

Where did Rinehart get those facts for his log?

From me, that's where. I'd been telling him all month about my hopes for the season. He'd copied down my dreams along with his white-mice experiments and salamander drawings, all mixed together.

"Watch Zan make a long throw from deep in the hole." Rinehart gestured to me with his log. He stabbed his pen toward our outfielders, who were shagging Coach's muddy flies. "They never miss," Rinehart claimed. "And notice Fritz working with Randy's curveball. Those two know each other's moves."

Mr Mergler watched where Rinehart pointed. And everywhere else on the Generals' field that first day of baseball practice, until it got too dark for reporters but not dark enough to stop us from running a lap of our track, other side of the fence. Us infielders moved four abreast. We elbowed each other and pushed for fun. Then, arms coiled around each other, we headed into our locker room. To untape our ankles. To soak in the whirlpool. To relax in the steam bath and pass around a Pepsi. Us infielders stick together.

Chapter 2

Tuesday morning dragged while I waited for base-ball practice. In homeroom I squeezed a tennis ball to strengthen my throwing hand. I raised and lowered the windows ten times each to loosen my shoulders. No sense wasting time during roll call. My legs felt weak. I used excuses to exercise them. Like jog to the trash basket. Jog down the rows, borrowing a pencil and paper. Jog the long way around to collect absentee slips. Barrel down to the office, turn them in, sprint back through empty halls to hear morning announcements.

"Attention. Attention. This is your principal with important information for the Robert E. Lee student body."

Squeeze. Bounce the ball off my feet and catch those bad hops.

"Lee's varsity baseball team will be photographed for the yearbook this afternoon before practice. Members—wear your pinstripes with dignity."

Never mind pictures. How about our schedule of exhibition games. I'll copy them down for Rinehart in case he can creep away from his experimental animals those afternoons.

The principal continued. "Our very own Generals will open the season with practice games against Prince William County and Front Royal High."

"Never heard of either," I told anyone in earshot. "We'll trounce 'em." I bounced and caught and didn't listen anymore. Who cared about spring prom queens? Who cared what the lunch menu was? Our team ate special training food at a table all our own. And we couldn't attend the annual band concert because of our training schedule—asleep by 9:00 P.M. Coach's orders. Doesn't give me much time for homework.

When announcements stopped I snuck out of homeroom and ran to English before the halls filled up. I dodged counselors, the librarian, and other hall monitors. I didn't want to knock anyone down with my clumsy base path style. "Clumsy," I told myself, bumping upstairs. Lucky most running around on the diamond is free of obstacles except when a baseman tries to tag your head. Or some big catcher tries to block your slide to the plate.

I slid into my seat next to Rinehart. He always beats me to first period. He unsnapped his briefcase and handed me my English text. He hauled my books around to underline the important parts. Plus he wanted to save my energy for shortstopping.

"What's this, Rinehart?" I whispered about two crisp sheets of typing he placed carefully on my desk while Miss Harrison asked, "Who's absent?"

"No one, ma'am. I've already counted," Rinehart answered her in his sweetest voice, the one he saved for scheming. He was covering up for Aileen, our left fielder. "She's probably sleeping late. Her beauty rest for the team picture," he wrote on a note and passed it.

15

I settled back for the English lesson. We'd spent all fall on eight parts of speech—two parts per month. Winter we'd learned the punctuation marks—two per month. Now we were up to essays, "putting it all together," Fuzzy Harrison lectured. We'd named her "Fuzzy" because of her hair. And head. "Using the fascinating words you've striven so hard to master and their valuable aides—commas, semicolons—uh—"

"Dash," volunteered Rinehart.

"Exclamation point, my favorite," I reminded her.

"Wonderful, well, using these tools for better expression, you will compose one essay each week until May, when you will compose book reports." She turned to the blackboard and printed

> My Hobby
> My Best Friend
> My Most Embarrassing Moment
> What I Did Last Summer

"These are the subjects for your next assignment. Now hand in the essay due today."

I craned my neck to see the list over her hair. "Don't bother," whispered Rinehart. "You'll strain yourself for baseball. I'll be writing them for you anyway." He tapped his pen on the typed sheets he'd given me. "Read your first essay."

I glanced at the top page. I noticed he'd signed my name, upper right-hand corner. My own scrawl. Then he'd typed the title and around a million more words.

"Precisely five hundred words, Fuzzy's assignment. She grades on words." Rinehart didn't whisper because Fuzzy was answering class questions pretty loud.

"Yes, spelling counts. Yes, ink must be black. Typing is better. No, you cannot think up your own subjects."

I held my ears and read Rinehart's forgery.

MY FAVORITE PET

My favorite pet is a newt I captured at Lubber Run Park one fine morning last autumn. I named my newt Dorothy Harrison in honor of my positively favorite English teacher I've studied with in all my school years.

My newt is speckled and lovely. I have taught him (or her) numerous tricks (described in detail below), and I plan to enter him (or her) in the science fair in an effort to defeat Arthur Rinehart, who wins every time.

Right around then I broke out laughing. I happened to know that this particular newt died last month. Rinehart pickled him or her in a Tang jar. I also believed that Fuzzy would never fall for his forgery. "Rinehart, everyone at Lee High understands that in spring season my *only* pet is my baseball glove." I patted mine where he'd fixed the laces. I stroked the majorettes' autographs in the pocket: Ruby Jean Twilly. DeeDee Tupper. Every finger of my pet Wilson glove had teammates' signatures,

17

front and back: Monk. Ben. Aileen. DumDum. Randy. E.J. Fritz. Jumbo. I touched the names. Ink counts for sure. I put my head down on my glove and tried to sleep until the bell rang.

Rinehart turned my newt essay in to Fuzzy. I couldn't face her Walking to chorus, he schemed about my other assignments. "Here's what," he said over the racket. "I'll type just one long essay—two thousand words. In it I'll cover all four titles. Hmmmm. Listen to this: WHAT I DID LAST SUMMER WITH MY BEST FRIEND WHO WAS MY MOST EMBARRASSING HOBBY

In chorus, before we sang, I had time to say, "Won't work on Fuzzy." Going to science, I explained why. "Because what I did last summer was throw my baseball a hundred thousand times against the garage door—at square targets I painted. First base. Second base. I stood on different cracks in the pavement way back to Military Road. Throwing's no hobby. That's my life. And my best friend wasn't there to embarrass me. You were locked in your dumb laboratory weighing birds' eggs."

"Fuzzy didn't see what you were really doing." Rinehart waved, on his way to advanced-placement biology.

She'll see soon enough if she reads Ronald Mergler's sports column or watches TV when we win the state series. Our baseball season will tell her the truth. I slunk into my lowly general science class.

I hate science. It's my only subject worse than badminton in gym class: I can't stand a game played with feathers. And science—I can't understand gravity or the laws of motion even when Rinehart explains them in sports terms. Like about balls in the air— what goes up comes down. "You're a genius," I tell him, "but fly balls aren't science. They're about quick feet, good hands, concentrating your brain, and no sun in your eyes." If I correct him on gravity, Rinehart moves right along to parts of the body. I'm supposed to sketch a skeleton for science. Memorize muscles. Name all the bones and junk in between them on the final exam this semester. I'll probably fail.

From habit today I read during science while the other kids scribbled Dr. Semler's words. I hid behind my book—*Play Winning Baseball* by Coach Michael O'Hara—so Dr. Semler wouldn't call on me. He didn't. He'd given up the week I handed in my term paper on spheres. "Spheres are balls," was the only sentence I'd written. On the next nineteen pages I'd drawn golf balls and tennis balls and basketballs and fifteen others. What failed me was the football. Rinehart hadn't explained quite enough.

Lunch bell finally rang, and I slipped through the mob, careful not to squash my throwing arm. At the cafeteria door I saw my teammates lined up. Aileen, her long hair in perfect curls, led the parade to our own special platesful of training food. Rare steak today. I could smell it. Nothing but the best for us Generals. Coach O'Hara had thought of every detail to make us winners. We were ordered to eat slowly and sit together to talk baseball strategy. We looked like a secret club, us in our separate corner.

"Hey, Zan," called Monk.

"Hey yourself," I answered, feeling right at home first time all morning.

"Sit by me," E.J. said. "By me," Monk said. "By us."

Our table had water pitchers and extra napkins, our own mustard in squirters so we didn't need to rewait in line. No one came near us except Lurleen Dewey to ask what cheers we wanted her to lead our first game. And Rae Ann Tupper brought her boyfriend a paper bag.

"Junk food! Don't eat that, DumDum!" Eugene warned him.

"Ah, Matello, turn loose my Fritos. They help a guy's batting average."

"Count your calories, DumDum. You've got all kinds of help on your plate."

DumDum wiped grease away. He held some fingers up, some down. "I can only count ten. The steak meat went for more."

"Steak, five hundred." Eugene wrote his calories in a notebook. He was trying to diet. "Carrying extra weight makes me tired. Tired legs are slow legs," he chanted to himself, the way Coach taught him. E.J. polished off Eugene's applesauce cake. For sure she wouldn't gain weight.

Aileen shook her curls. "If I ate two desserts I'd swell up like Babe Ruth's stomach."

"You play the same position as Babe. Why not?" Ben asked.

"Because I don't want to be just your typical average outfielder. I'm hoping to be Robert E. Lee prom queen, too."

20

"Is that why you wore these girlie curls?" Randy pulled one out straight, let go, and it snapped right back in place.

Aileen said, "Meany. I curled my hair to be ready for our team picture today. And I wore this." She showed us her ankle bracelet under the table.

"That'll go awful with your baseball shoes. A gold chain and silver spikes? I thought girls weren't supposed to mix gold and silver." Randy didn't act completely disgusted. He knew better than to make fun of a teammate. He needed every run she could score to help him become the league's MVP—most valuable pitcher. He said, "Tell you what, Aileen. This whole gang will vote you prom queen if you steal a base per game until then."

"Great idea," E.J. agreed.

DumDum uncrooked his fingers from around his milk. "I'll vote this many times if you put your hex jinx on the Redskins. What gets me is how they beat us in the series last year."

Our team suddenly seemed grim with the memory: Redskins, 2 games to 1. Eugene hammered the table. Randy laid his fork down and never took another bite. Monk wiped his eyes with a napkin. No one spoke until Aileen said, "Meanies!" meaning the Redskins this time.

"Wait'll next year—we'll get even with Joe Donn Joiner," DumDum predicted.

"This is next year," Ben reminded him.

"Yeah," said Randy. "I'll beanball Joiner."

"Yeah," said Fritz. "I'll tag him where it hurts."

I couldn't think what to promise for our innings

against Joe Donn, so I chipped in my best friend for our other cause. I said, "Rinehart will scheme how to stuff the ballot box for Aileen, no problem. He knows about numbers. Our left fielder's good as prom queen now."

"And the Redskins are Deadskins if we play our best game," Monk reassured us as we stood up, stretched, and grabbed our gear from a private shelf above our table. We left the cafeteria together for classes.

"See ya soon," Monk said. He touched his glove to mine. We both wore them around a lot to get used to the weight on our hands.

That afternoon dragged slower than all morning. During American history I bounced my ball on the desk at the same time as I answered questions on a pop quiz. I wrote "True" in half the blanks, changed hands, and put "True" in the other half. I'm a switch writer, I told myself. I wish I could also be a switch hitter. I might get more raps off Joe Donn Joiner. I wish he'd play fair. I wished away the rest of history. I wished for faster legs. For larger hands. I could make mine stronger but not bigger. Maybe they'd grow by the year I'm a senior.

In math class I really settled down to business. While everyone else measured angles I took my ruler and drew the Generals' home baseball field to scale. I marked each guy's defensive position. I noted distances between bases and between the pitcher's mound and the plate. Those are numbers, aren't they? And I'm in math, aren't I? When I finished my drawing I hunched over it, pushing a scrap of paper from base to base. Once I glanced up at the wall clock. How long should it take this runner to move these ninety feet to first base from home? Why doesn't the clock have a sweep-second hand? How can I run faster on real base paths?

"Like every other sports skill—work at it," Rinehart told me in study hall, where he watched me play my baseball game.

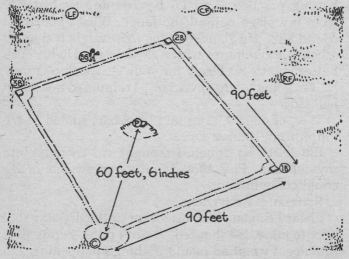

I moved my paper base runner faster and faster. I pretended it was me against Joe Donn Joiner, one on one. Rinehart answered all my questions with "Work." He said, "Work at making sharp turns while you round bases. Make sure your foot hits that inside corner of the bag. And push hard in the direction of the next bag. Lean your body toward the pitcher, lowering your left shoulder. Run on the balls of your feet for proper spring and balance. Run in a straight line—"

"Hold it, Rinehart. Where did you learn this technical advice about a game you fail in gym class every year?"

Rinehart answered, as cool as a major leaguer in an iced-tea ad, "I listened to Mr. O'Hara yesterday. He was coaching DumDum while you infielders took batting practice. And I'll be listening again today from my place behind the fence. What's your best friend for?" He glanced at his wristwatch. It showed seconds and minutes with a gleaming red light. "You better run to get ready for your yearbook picture."

"I'm going to my physician," I reminded the study-hall lady.

"Yes, of course," she said. Rinehart smiled in triumph from the last row.

Rinehart's no slouch, I thought as I changed into my uniform. Plus that scientist wristwatch of his could come in handy.

Rrrrrrang. Rrrrrrrang.

I heard Eugene kick his locker in the dressing stall next to mine. He shouted, "I can't drink Pepsis after practice. I weighed in and nothing's happening. I'm same as yesterday."

"Take a haircut," Fritz yelled across the locker room.

"You'll soon lose weight if you stay on Coach's diet," E.J. called down the line. "Don't kick your locker. We need you at third."

Eugene kicked his dressing stool. I always knew when he was suiting up. I couldn't see him but I sure could hear. We all were assigned private spaces with curtains separating us. We had slots for our books, shelves for towels and clean socks, pegs for our school clothes and dressing robes. Our names were painted on wide gray lockers. In there we hung our warm-up jackets and three uniforms: home-game white uniforms with navy-blue pinstripes; away-game blue ones with white pinstripes; and our practice uniform, mostly mud brown. I kept my spikes on the bottom shelf. I tugged them on now, grateful to Buddy. When we were in the steam room yesterday he'd gone through our lockers and polished ten pairs of shoes. He'd also left me a batter's helmet that fit.

No one fooled around in our locker room today. Teammates crowded the mirrors, combing their hair. Eugene couldn't make his lie down. He jammed on his cap to cover up. He tried some hair spray under the brim. Aileen's long red curls reached the name on her uniform: A. Dickerson. She wouldn't wear her cap to "muss up." Monk tucked his St. Christopher medal under his shirt, pulled it out—in—out. "The camera won't notice," he said to our smiles in the mirror. "Let's get this picture over with so's we can play us some ball," said Fritz.

"Will the camera be big enough for our mighty Generals?" I asked. I saluted my mates.

Randy led us out to the bleachers. Coach O'Hara met us there and arranged us perfect. Me, Monk, Randy, Fritz, E.J., Eugene, and Jumbo Williams, our relief pitcher, sitting down. Aileen, Ben, DumDum, Coach O'Hara, Buddy, and Dr. Ableson, our team trainer, kneeling above us. Our cocaptains, Randy

25

and Fritz, waved crossed bats. Us others held our gloves in our laps. Aileen untwisted her ankle bracelet. Monk crossed himself. Eugene sucked in his cheeks.

"Say 'Cheese,' " said the photographer.

We didn't say "Cheese." We said, "CHAMPS."

Chapter 3

Sunny Wednesday and a private lesson with Coach.

He called me to a huddle with E.J. and Aileen. He said, "During tryouts last weekend I judged on your fielding and batting. That you can do. Now I must discover how well you three rookies run the bases. Exhibition season is only a week away. You'll have to learn fundamentals by the Prince William game. My Generals are known as a running team."

I kept my eyes down on home plate, afraid Coach could read my mind. I'd caught balls off the garage door and hit doubles in Military Road, but I'd never practiced running on a real baseball diamond. In gym class we played softball on a scabby field. Our teacher wouldn't let us steal bases or slide. We might ruin our gym suits or ourselves.

"I already know how," Aileen piped up. She wasn't afraid of Coach. "My boyfriend showed me. Every summer at Ocean City we play games on the beach."

Coach let his breath out in surprise. He barked, "Dickerson, beach ball isn't Virginia League baseball." He handed her a bat. "I want you to swing, pretend you've connected, run the bases with a slide into third. I'll time you with this." He uncupped a handful of stopwatch.

I didn't look up when Aileen swung and ran. I

27

believed her. I happened to know her boyfriend, a star for St. Vincent's Prep. That guy would always want to win, even pickup games at a clambake. He'd have taught Aileen plenty. Still, I listened for Coach to holler instructions. He always found details that a player could improve.

"Fine," he called to Aileen. "Return to first base."

E.J. added, "Great slide."

Coach challenged Aileen again. "I want you to steal second this time. I'll be the opposing catcher. Johnston, take your usual position at first. Give the pitcher a target to throw at on the pickoff. Hold the runner close. Hagen here will pitch to me." He ran his fingers through his crew cut. That meant business.

I went out to the mound and business began. Aileen took a lead off first. I threw to E.J. Aileen dived back safe. She stood up on the bag and wiped her hands carefully along her pants. E.J. threw me the ball and Aileen took a bigger lead. I threw to E.J., but not before Aileen got back safe. She said, "Time out." She moved behind the bag. She retied her shoelaces in their usual floppy bows. She examined her fingernail polish. She said, "Time in." She watched me watch her take a small lead. What should I do? I decided to pitch. Yes, pitch. No, don't. Aileen now had a lead so huge I thought I could pick her off. I burned one over to E.J. while Aileen went for the bag.

"Safe," Coach called.

I waited for him to say more. Like hurry up with this game. Quit goofing around. He said, "Play ball."

Aileen led off first about three and a half steps. I decided to ignore her. I'd seen that dance before. And those eye-shadowy eyes. I gave her one more glance just in case. She leaned toward second with a sly grin. I thought about throwing to E.J. I thought about pitching to Coach. I threw my fastest ball yet to E.J.

Aileen didn't wait to hear "Safe." She was sure. She called, "Time out" and smoothened every wrinkle in her uniform. She drummed her foot on the bag. "I'm really stealing this time," she told me.

"So you say," I was dumb enough to brag.

"Play ball," Coach commanded.

Aileen's lead wasn't all that big. I concentrated on my pitch. I didn't want to throw the ball away—into the screen. Okay, ready or not, I'm pitching. After a nod to Coach. After wondering if— After catching a peripheral blur of Aileen heading—

Heading anywhere, it couldn't matter by then. I'd flung the ball past E.J., into Row 25 of the bleachers. Aileen never slowed up at second base. She came all the way home and hugged Coach.

He didn't hug back but he wasn't exactly mad at her, either. He said, "Just one or two things I want you to know." He nodded at me. "Hagen isn't an experienced pitcher. Her moves are less than refined. Ordinarily you'll want to take a slightly shorter lead."

"Sure." Aileen spoke right up. "I was studying Zan's rhythm. Head, shoulders, feet. I always study the pitcher. Reflexes. That. Like my boyfriend told me." She twirled a curl. "Any more?"

Coach smiled, first time this season. "You lost your ankle bracelet rounding third." He gave E.J. the bat. "Next."

Calmly E.J. swung, let go the bat, ran the bases swifter than Aileen. She touched the front of each bag. She stayed smoothly on the paths. She pretended to watch the coach at third who'd be giving her signals in a real game. She didn't take a chance at home. She slid. Without brushing herself off, she answered Coach's question. "I played at camp. We used boys' rules."

Coach stared down at me. "And Hagen, I suppose you're about to admit that you've been trained to run, steal, and slide by the old Brooklyn Dodgers?"

"Ummm."

"Did I miss again? Ty Cobb?" Coach scowled his usual.

"Ummm. I read a lot," I said, remembering Coach's book I'd reviewed in science. I'd also memorized the stealing pictures. When Coach didn't answer, I mumbled, "Anyway, I can throw hard."

Coach didn't mention bleachers. He'd already sent Buddy under them to collect my wild pickoff. Coach waved E.J. and Aileen to the batter's cage. He timed me once around the bases. He led me alone to first base. He said, "The value of an act like Dickerson's is that she upsets the pitcher—any pitcher, not only you. With Dickerson on base, pitchers will lose their concentration. They'll worry, look, throw, look. She's harassing them. A pitcher will walk the batter he's facing or serve up a fat pitch for a homer. Also, she keeps a first baseman pinned close to the bag. That

leaves a bigger hole here for the batter to slap one."
He pointed past me and into right field.

All this made sense.

"Dickerson learned her lesson well. She studied your moves. She watched you for a break. She had the good jump. She knows how to slide. And those red ringlets—opposing players will be disconcerted for various reasons."

I felt my own short hair, all full of dirt from my bumpy slide home. I wasn't about to win games on looks. I'd have to be faster. Slidier. Coach walked me to second with this warning: "When you steal, you slide. When you slide, you hurt. Some part of you always hurts at least for a few minutes afterward. Your hands sting. Your legs smart. You get calf bruises, scrapes. You can be spiked by the player defending his base. Ankles. Wrists."

My chest still felt sore from Monday's collision with the ball. My knee still felt twisted after yesterday's crash into Monk. We'd both chased the same fly. And true, my hands still stung from my only slide ever. I rubbed them along my pants, the way I'd seen Aileen do. Maybe she knows a trick about pain. No, about dirt. My clean hands stung. I said, "I'm ready."

Coach called for Buddy. He asked him to bring two golf gloves. He made me put these on. He said, "Whenever there's a close play at this base—and third—and home—you slide. By diving headfirst you can get here faster than feet first. I'll demonstrate slow motion." He trotted to first base, turned, trotted toward second. I jumped off the bag to make room. He launched out from his trot, his body like a big

31

bullet. He didn't pull a belly whopper. He slid along the dirt on his forearms and elbows. At the base he popped up, ready to run again. "In case the ball gets by the second baseman. Your turn, Hagen."

My turn lasted the rest of Wednesday's practice. While the other kids hit baseballs, I hit the dirt. Headfirst. Shoulder first until Coach showed me again. Golf gloves first. Wrists first. Once even nose first. I smelled canvas. But only a split second. Pop up, try again. Forearms first. Forearms first. I broke my dive by learning to land on my forearms and knees. Ouch.

And just as I started to feel comfortable being a bullet, Coach said, "Enough."

Whew!

"Now the hook slide—the conventional slide in our league. Let's try home for a change."

I followed Coach in from second base. He demonstrated until home plate disappeared under dirt from his spikes. I listened to his corrections as I slid and slid and slid.

"Stay low. Stay low going into your slide. Only your buttocks should touch the ground." Coach spanked me exactly where I should land.

I landed enough times to rub a hole in the seat of my practice uniform.

"Fold your arms against your body. Keep them off the ground to prevent injury."

What arms? Oh, you mean these raggy sleeves? I couldn't feel bones in them. Parts of me paralyzed. I lay on my back, waiting for stars to come out. It must be night. I couldn't hear cheerleaders practicing anymore. I couldn't hear doubles zapping out of the cage. But right above me I heard Coach calling his Generals to their positions. Coach didn't help me up. I leaped up when he said, "Hagen will run bases under game conditions. Boyle, pitch her something hittable. Buddy, give her a drink."

Buddy gave me a bat. Fritz took his place behind me and signaled Randy. He threw my favorite pitch. With an exhausted swing I tapped a weak grounder. Easy out.

I dumped my bat and ran for first anyway, quick as I could churn my stumps. I didn't watch the ball because "watching costs speed," I remembered from Coach's book. I hoped for a fielder's error. I crossed the bag with an extra spurt.

"She's alive," came Rinehart's voice. I hadn't heard him since study hall.

"Safe," Coach shouted from where he substituted at my position. He'd bobbled my grounder, probably on purpose. He held the ball and gave orders.

So there I was a runner. Jumbo Williams would try to move me over with a hit. I'd also move myself. I stopped searching the faces at the fence for Rinehart. I paid closer attention to Randy than he paid himself. He pitched to Jumbo—ball one. He juggled the catch from Fritz and waited. He bluffed me back to first with a look. He wiped his face on his shirttail. He pitched again without his usual concentration. He seemed tired. His fastball traveled half speed. My legs were too sore to worry him worse with a dance. I stayed put on the bag, noticing Randy's fastball get slower. Jumbo fouled three off, four off. Randy's ball took longer and longer to reach home plate.

I stole second base on that slow ball. Fritz couldn't throw to second until he caught the pitch. The pitch didn't hurry. I hurried. I slid under Monk's tag.

"Safe at second," Coach said right near me.

Safe but numb from one too many slides. I'd never make it to third unless Jumbo hit the ball to China. Then I'd crawl those ninety feet.

Jumbo bunted. The ball sputtered down the third-base line. Heavy-footed, I held my bag. I saw Eugene stab the bunt with his bare hand. In one motion he threw to first ahead of Jumbo. Beautiful throw, but Eugene fell down making it. With no one else near third, I decided to run there. "Legs, just this dinky ninety feet," I promised mine. By the time Eugene arrived to take E.J.'s peg I was standing up on his base. Obviously safe. Coach didn't call. Eugene didn't kick. He seemed too tired for anger.

"Who wants to knock Hagen home?" Coach asked his fading players.

No volunteers on that twilit field. Nothing but groans.

"Then I'll do it." Coach tossed his glove to Buddy. "Will you cover shortstop?" he asked our equipment manager, the most uncoordinated guy in the stadium besides Arthur Rinehart. I'd finally spotted Rinehart perched in the bleachers. He was checking me out with a telephoto lens.

Coach patted Randy's first pitch straight back to the mound. Randy caught it clean on one hop and threw to E.J. for another easy out.

Except *I* wasn't out. Soon as Randy had gone into

his windup I'd broken for home. Not because I wanted to show off my hook slide. Not because I needed to score the winning run. Never mind heroes. I wanted to rest my legs. Sit down. Fall down in a slide under E.J.'s throw to Fritz guarding the plate. Fritz had the ball. Fritz tried to tag me. I slid into his shin guards harder than the whole afternoon put together. Fritz held the ball and I was "Out."

"I'm lying here until tomorrow's practice," I groaned to the Generals gathering around to unsnarl us.

"Nifty slide," Coach admitted. "Don't hesitate to use it in games."

"Whatever—to win," Monk praised me.

Ben and DumDum lifted me on their shoulders. "We'll ride you to the showers," Ben said. On the way there DumDum told me, "You done splendid."

Chapter 4

All week long we stole, slid, threw, caught, fielded, batted, bunted, ran, walked, swung, and hit, hit, hit. Eugene lost weight. Ben stopped ducking the curve. Fritz and Randy worked on their signals so other teams couldn't steal them. Aileen learned the suicide squeeze. Monk and E.J. practiced rundown plays between their bases. Jumbo pitched sliders in the bull pen. I hit the fastball, hit to opposite fields, hit sacrifice flies, hit homers. DumDum roved right field calling numbers to us Generals: "One out, two to go. Monk, do a double play. Two balls, no strikes—look out, Eugene for the bunt. One man on first. One batter up. One out. If I catch a fly, I throw to second."

No time-outs until Sunday.

Then I stayed in my room and finished up homework. For math I drew parallelograms, not diamonds. For English I reread *Play Winning Baseball*. I planned to write my book report on it in May. The plot seemed easy. The characters all are my friends. There's only one theme—winning. Fuzzy will love it. I phoned Rinehart to discuss my idea. No answer.

After lunch I struggled through a confusing science chapter, this one about vital organs. When I came to the end and couldn't find arms, my vitalest organs, I tried Rinehart again for an explanation. No answer.

I took my glove, bat, and balls to the driveway for practice. I threw overhand at my first-base target on the garage door. Fifty throws. One hundred. I moved farther back. I threw sidearm, caught the ball on bad hops from cracked cement. I moved in close to bunt at my third-base target. I bunted left-handed, right-handed. I moved to the backyard for slugging practice. I strung my usual tennis ball to the clothesline and swung at it for an hour. Most of that time I spent untangling the ball I'd powdered for triples and homers. I hit plastic balls off my batting tee, chased them to the neighbor's yard, and hit them again.

Now I needed someone to knock me fungoes in the street. I thought of E.J., but I knew she'd be writing her essay for Fuzzy. Monk goes to afternoon Mass. Randy hates to hit. Rinehart can't hit, but I'm phoning him all the same. I can practice backing him up while he lets baseballs bounce through his legs.

"Rinehart, come on over and be my designated bungler," I said when he answered.

"You come here to the movies." He invited me in his scheming voice.

Movies? What next from Rinehart's laboratory? I wondered along Glebe Road.

Down in the basement everything seemed like usual. The same white mice gnawed their health food. The same Bunsen burner heated a test tube full of icky gunk. Snakes under glass slept a lot. The incubator and calculator and film developer and scales and duplicator were waiting for Rinehart's next experiment. His different cameras sat on shelves. He typed another minute on his favorite machine and handed me the results. "Your essay," he said. "Turn it in tomorrow."

I read his title: MY MOST EMBARRASSING FRIEND LAST SUMMER. "Rinehart, you left out 'hobby,'" I reminded my forger.

"Hmmm." He uncapped his pen and rewrote: MY BEST HOBBY EMBARRASSED MY FRIEND ALL LAST SUMMER.

"Lookit—'best' goes with 'friend,' not 'hobby.' This is hopeless."

"Nothing's hopeless to a man of science. Give it here."

He typed like a fiend for ten minutes. I inspected jars full of ex-pets. I tiptoed around looking for a book to read, one about arms, not spleens. I fed a cough drop from Rinehart's medical bag to his man-eating plant. It wilted some. Then I got bored in the lab. I should have brought my glove to oil with Rinehart's all-purpose recipe he called Mung. I should swing my bat in front of his trick mirror. But I'd better not swing near these shelves. I could cause a flood of formaldehyde. Or release a jillion chiggers.

Rinehart finally unrolled my essay from his typewriter. I read his title. He was right. Nothing's hopeless. "What part does your newt play in all this?" I asked to keep him semihumble.

"Remember last Friday? Fuzzy already gave our first essay an A on him."

"Or her. Where's the movies you promised?"

I expected enlargements of moths for the science fair or a set of colored slides. Turtles. Pigeons.

Rinehart's lab went suddenly dark. He must

have pressed a hidden switch. He must be pressing another because around me I heard buzzes. Not insects, either. More like motors. My eyes didn't have time to adjust and see the screen before a light blazed on it. With another faint click, a real movie began. Rinehart said, "It's my first human film. It's silent."

I saw myself, not a lizard. "Whew—that's me up there in the batter's cage. Taking my cuts."

"Zan swings, Zan hits. Swings, hits. Swing, bam." Rinehart made "bam" sound like my bat.

I loved the narration. I watched myself using my favorite bat, a lightweight Louisville Slugger. I'd shined it for hours. I'd rubbed stickum on the handle to help my grip. I treated my bat like a baby. I never let it lie around on damp ground. A bat will pick up moisture. Get heavier. I want mine to weigh the same thirty-one ounces every time I swing.

"Swing—boom. Swing—boom."

"Rinehart, I'm not up there just swinging. I'm thinking. I'm trying not to be distracted by how my bruises hurt."

"Where are they? I'll put Mung on them for a total cure."

"Also I'm concentrating on the pitch. I'm not letting myself feel how my uniform pinches across the shoulders."

"Ask Mr. O'Hara for a bigger shirt."

"And what would you make me do about this beanball Randy throws?"

Rinehart stopped the projector right where I fell back on my heels. He peered at the film. "You did it—you dodged. But why does your own teammate try to conk you?"

"Go figure it. You're the schemer. See, there—Randy tried again. Coach O'Hara made him brush me back. I can use the practice. Not in ducking. That's a cinch. But every batter needs to get up again, take the same batting stance as before, and face a pitcher without fear, or at least without showing fear. Fear of being hit can ruin a baseball player."

Rinehart rewound the film. He reran it to where Randy hit the brim of my batter's helmet and spun it on my head. He shivered. He turned on the lights. "Such bravery calls for a cookie," he announced, going to his medicine cabinet. He passed me a box of wheat-germ newtons he'd made in his sterilizer oven. I munched to be polite, to thank Rinehart for saving me from a Sunday without my team. I pretended to myself I was eating liver, which tasted better. I swallowed. "Great flavor," I said, sounding like E.J.

"I know you prefer Hydrox, but these are more nourishing for sports strength. My mice fed on wheat germ outrun my mice that eat chocolate store-bought cookies."

I ate another homemade cookie, hoping my legs would get its message. Rinehart opened cans of film. He held up strips to the light. "I took these with a telephoto lens from the bleachers. Humans are difficult to photograph, but somehow they developed better than my butterfly science project last year."

"That's because athletes ace out bugs," said I with my mouth clear of icky cookies. I'd swallowed hard.

"Next feature. Do you want to see all your other Generals at bat?"

I did. And I knew my teammates would want to. So we manned Rinehart's phone. We convinced half the team to spend an evening admiring each other on film. Until curfew at 9:00 P.M. "Better bring your own refreshments," I warned the ones who wouldn't like liver. I stacked gerbil cages to make room for our audience. Rinehart brought chairs from upstairs. He crammed these in front of his workbench near the screen. While we waited, he finished boiling a row of beakers and poured the gunk in a canister, full. "Mung," he murmured. "Cure anything." Smoke curled around his head.

"Smells like the Colonel down here," DumDum said. He'd ridden over with Aileen. "It's not your typical average theater," she agreed. "Ech. I won't sit next to a rat." She flounced off that chair and onto another, okay until she saw toads. "I'm standing up," she said.

Ben and Fritz didn't mind. They said "Hello" to every cage. They tilted their chairs, feet on the workbench. They settled down among the animals like a couple more guinea pigs. They even ate Rinehart's cookies. "Didja see that?" Fritz asked and gave a roar of delight when Aileen beat out a bunt on the screen. "She drove the pitcher nuts."

Before her bunt Aileen had done about nineteen things in the on-deck circle and nineteen more before she stood in the batter's box. No one ever used so many wiggles on sleeves. By the time they were perfect, Aileen bent to make sure her ankle bracelet faced the plate. Then readjust sleeves. Take off her batter's helmet and check the padding. Unsnap her suede batter's glove. Resnap. Blow on her fingers.

"This is it, Queenie."

Not yet. Aileen still had to chat with the catcher. Re-readjust her sleeves. Step into the box. Step out for a glance at her pants. Are they up too high in the waist?

"We're ready, babe," Fritz said.

Dirty? No, not a speck. Dust off pants, anyway. Shine her boyfriend's class ring with spit. Step into the box. Flash a grin at the pitcher. Relax into usual stance but pull a surprise. Get ready fast to bunt. Pivot to face pitcher. Slide top hand up bat handle to the trademark. Move bat in front of body. Keep bat parallel to the ground. Still grinning, look straight ahead. Bunt top half of the ball so it goes on the ground, not up for a fly. Bunt right back to the unsuspecting pitcher. Dash to beat his angry throw.

"Aileen, you're a natural lead-off batter," hollered Fritz to our actress on first base. Aileen sat down close beside him when he said, "You're hard to pitch to. You'll get lotsa bases on balls from rattled pitchers. You sprint like a bunny. Wait'll Joe Donn Joiner gets a load of you jiggling. He'll go bananas." Fritz cracked his red knuckles in glee.

Rinehart balanced his log on his knees beside the projector. He asked Fritz, "Who'd make a good second batter in your lineup, Captain? I'll run that film."

"Our Monk hit second other years. To me it's a tossup between him and Hagen."

Those two films didn't take long. I heard Rinehart

whisper, "Zan-boom!" as I connected. Fritz analyzed each of us, ending, "They both hit well to right field, both have good batting averages from our squad games. Monk is better at the hit-and-run play. I gotta think. Yeah, I gotta give the edge to Monk on running and experience. He helped win big games for us last year."

DumDum said, "Nope, not *the* biggie."

"The whole team choked in the series, not just Monk. Joe Donn psyched us out." Ben refused another cookie, remembering out loud.

The basement gloom was so thick the mice quit eating, too. Silent in the dark, we plotted revenge. "There's a lot of get-backing in sports," I informed Rinehart for his log. He took notes about our feelings. After a while he said, "Cheer up. I'm not showing soap operas tonight. Who's your third batter in the lineup, Captain?"

Fritz slapped the guy next to him. "Ben Brown— best hitter on the team. Combines distance with average. If the first two players do their jobs and get on base, Ben'll bring them around. Then our cleanup batter oughtta swat everybody home."

"Me," DumDum said proudly. "I'm number four." He held up three fingers.

Ben and DumDum starred in two reels of power hitting. Ben squared his shoulders the exact same way each time in his stance. He waited for "his" pitch and went for it with a flat swing. Once he fell sprawling away from a beanball Randy had thrown at him for practice. Zoop, down Ben went. Zip, up in a hurry. He stepped in and planted his foot. "I'm really

43

afraid," he confessed to his audience. "That ball's coming at me ninety-five miles an hour. But this year the Redskins won't know how I feel." The next pitch he let hit his sleeve.

"I ain't afraid," DumDum said. He proved it by crowding the plate like a buffalo. His muscles bulged, giving the pitcher targets he didn't have with skinny Aileen and me.

"Hang in there," Fritz hollered to the film Dum-Dum.

"Challenge that pitcher," Ben whispered as if to tell himself.

I felt Rinehart shiver in the chair beside me. "Wicked game," he said over the hum of his projector. "I wonder why humans play it? Rats wouldn't— except for food."

DumDum dug in and swung at every ball thrown in his direction. The nearer the better. The farther the better. His strike zone was any inch his fat bat could reach with a whooooosh. He hit high fastballs for homers. He hit low curves. He lined a slow outside pitch over the fence. DumDum's swing wasn't correct by any book. He seemed to have no eye for the perfect pitch and no rhythm. But he oozed confidence. Whooooosh. Thwack. I heard with no sound track on the film. Whooooosh. His casual swing sent fielders retreating to the bus stop. Ruby Jean Twilly caught his final blast in her megaphone.

"You didn't wince once," said Ben to his fellow outfielder. His compliment woke DumDum up. "What's the score? What's—oh, who's batting after me?"

Fritz continued with his lineup. "I bat fifth. I don't wantta see myself. I've been overstriding. Jerking my neck. Locking my hips. Holding my hands too high. I'm not getting good wood on the ball. I'm outa my groove." He waited until Rinehart wrote that down. "Wouldja show us Johnston?" asked Fritz. "She'll bat sixth from what I've seen her do so far. The sixth batter is like a second leadoff man. He often leads off in the second, fourth, or fifth innings. He's gotta be calm. Be a good clutch hitter to drive in runs. Be smart, hard to pitch to."

"That's E.J. all over," I said.

She didn't let me down. She stood in the box with eyes leveled on Randy, who pitched batting practice that day. He kept trying tricks to make her mad, to draw her attention off making solid contact. He threw the ball behind her. He closed his eyes and pitched with a windmill follow-through. He shouted at her when she wouldn't take his bait. He formed his hand and glove into a bullhorn, shouting again.

"What's he saying?" Rinehart asked. "I couldn't hear him that day from the bleachers."

"He's calling E.J. a sucker," we all answered.

E.J. waited in her stance.

"Are you going to let me call you a sucker?" Randy taunted.

E.J. shrugged. I could almost hear her pleasant laugh. "You'll get tired of it," she told her tormentor and sent his pitch into the distance.

Ben said, "She's not such a shabby batter up there in the movies. She gave Randy a lesson in cool. She's perfect as sixth."

"With Hagen seventh. The seventh guy should be like the second. Hagen could bat in either slot." Fritz left his seat. He cruised the basement looking for cookies. "Suppertime," he said to Rinehart.

Rinehart squinted at his wristwatch like some doctor taking pulse. "But not curfew. Eat gumdrops and conclude the lineup, Captain." He waved to his medical kit. "Candy in there."

Fritz shared a bottle of tar wads with us—at least, they chewed like tar. When the lights went out, I stuck mine under the workbench. With our teeth gummed together so we couldn't say a word, we watched Eugene's erratic batting. He lashed out at bad pitches. He paused and let strikes through the zone. He lengthened his stride. He shortened it. He hit a triple. He crouched. He straightened. He frowned at Randy and gripped the bat hard enough to squish it to sawdust. He spread his hands. He moved them closer together. He hit singles to left field and called time out. He loafed against the screen.

Fritz said, "Eugene can't find a comfortable stance. He better do it before the Prince William game this week or Coach'll bat him ninth, worse than Randy."

"Muscle hustle! What Eugene needs most. He's exhausted in the movies." Aileen put her coat on.

Rinehart shook his bottle of gumdrops. "Energy from these would make every General a champion."

"Ech. I wouldn't wish one on a deadly enemy."

"Hows about Joe Donn Joiner?"

"Send him the bottle special delivery. See ya tomorrow, Hagen."

"See ya."

"Our final practice before exhibitions. I'll be wearing my hitting clothes." I felt happy. I stayed with Rinehart to help feed his pets dinner. I unlocked cages. He offered gumdrops. His rats jumped for bites. I didn't know why. Couldn't their tongues taste? His gerbils gobbled. Frogs outhopped each other to reach Rinehart's outstretched hand. They weren't afraid of taste. They weren't afraid, period. I asked why.

"Oh, any number of possible reasons. They're hungry. They crave attention. Hmmmm. They're bored, otherwise, without interruptions. Hmmmm. Other motives . . ." Wise Rinehart seemed miles away, explaining. He puttered around the lab with a puzzled expression I'd hardly ever seen on him. As I started upstairs, he stopped me. He looked me over in a scientific way, head to foot, mostly arms. He might have been taking a picture just with his eyeball. Next he stared at his mice. He opened his log. He held a strip of film to the light, reviewing Generals swinging their bats. He asked, "Why do you hit balls? . . . See, here's how Monk pats you after your double. . . . That's your gumdrop. . . . But why do you stand waiting for the ball to hit you? . . . My mice know better. . . ."

I had no answer. How could a ball boomer explain to a ball misser? But I had a question. "Rinehart, what's in those nasty gumdrops?"

"It's my Mung, hardened into bite-sized balls." He

read from his log: "Specifically, chopped prunes and figs, wheat-germ oil, sesame seeds, carob powder, sunflower seeds, yogurt, brewers' yeast—"

"Rinehart, you're not to be believed."

"Yes I am."

Chapter 5

OFFICIAL BATTING ORDER
Robert E. Lee High School

Date 4 / 4

	ORIGINAL	POS.		CHANGE
1	Aileen Dickerson	LF	B	
			C	
2	John Cunningham	2B	B	
			C	
3	Ben Brown	CF	B	
			C	
4	Walter Cadden	RF	B	
			C	
5	Eugene Matello	3B	B	
			C	
6	Eleanor Johnston	1B	B	
			C	
7	Suzanne Hagen	SS	B	
			C	
8	Fritz Slappy	C	B	
			C	
9	Randolph Boyle	P	B	
			C	

Manager's Signature: *Michael O'Hara*

49

Chapter 6

"Play."

Umpires don't call, "Play ball," or at least not our umpire. He stuffed Coach's lineup card in his back pocket, brushed off home plate with his whisk broom, gave Fritz a new ball, and said, "Play."

The leadoff batter for Prince William hit Randy's first pitch for a single. Their second man walked on four straight balls. Their third man took three balls and two strikes, hit a long foul, hit a pop foul into the stands, and walked.

Bases loaded: first inning: opening game.

Fritz went out to the mound. He and Randy pushed dirt around with their spikes. They leaned close to each other, whispering. I strained to hear. Then I remembered I was on their same team—me, the shortstop. I could get into their huddle any old time I wanted to. In fact, I belonged there! I climbed to the top of our mound. I leaned in Randy's direction. My cap brim touched his. I whispered, "Bear down, fellow." I'd heard Coach say that.

"Lemme see that ball," Fritz said. He rubbed the seams with his big red hands. He flipped it to me and I rubbed. I also kicked dirt and chewed my gumdrop like a wad of tobacco. I checked the dugout in case Coach had a signal for us. He stood on the top step, hands jammed under his belt buckle. This was our signal for the double play. Fritz saw, too. He said, "Boyle, make their cleanup batter hit into a double play." He presented Randy the ball like a prize. We patted each other here and there and went back to our positions.

With the bases full of Princes, our Lee kids began chanting, "Deee-fense. Deee-fense." Ruby Jean and DeeDee held a bed sheet between them. They paraded it around until everyone, including us Generals, could read the three-foot-tall letters: LET'S GO, TEAM.

Let's go, Randy, I thought. He'd fallen behind, three balls, no strikes on the fourth batter.

"Strike one," called the umpire at last.

Randy looked in to his catcher for the sign. He shook off a first sign. Shook off a second. Then he went into his windup. He gripped the ball tight in his pitcher's glove. With his eyes glued on his target, he rocked back on his left foot. He brought his hands over his head, started them down, and kicked forward. All his force moved toward the plate as he delivered his fastball. His throwing arm almost wrapped around his body on the follow-through.

"Strike two."

The sound of that ball hitting Fritz's mitt could have been heard to Wilson Boulevard. When Randy turned to pick up the resin bag, I saw him grinning. Oh-oh. The show-off's gone to work. Randy's going to strike out the side. He shook off Fritz's next sign. He toed the rubber. He pumped, kicked, followed through—

"Strike. You're out."

Coach kept his hands under his belt buckle but Randy ignored all signs. He pitched *his* game. Pump. Kick. Follow-through. Strike. Pump. Kick. Follow-through. Strike. After the second batter struck out, Fritz called, "Time," trotted to the dugout, and came back with a sponge, which he slipped into his mitt. He returned to his crouch.

Wheesshh. The ball flew from Randy's strong arm. Pokkk!

"Strike." The umpire raised his right arm.

Wheesshh. Pokkk! "Ball one." Wheesshh. Pokkk! "Ball two." An even louder WHEESSHH while Randy's pitch traveled its sixty feet six inches to the plate. POKKK. Strikes and balls sounded so violent I thought Fritz might throw up his hands and hide. He'd need a mattress in his mitt at this rate. Meanwhile Randy wasn't even sweating. He didn't take deep breaths or fidget. He just threw—

"Strike three."

Our fielders had relaxed so much admiring Randy's effortless delivery we almost forgot to leave the diamond. We seemed hours getting to our dugout. Coach met us there, stern-faced. He chewed out Randy in front of us all. "You're not a movie star, Boyle. The mound's not your stage. You're part of a team that's out there to help you."

Aileen chose a bat and hurried to lead off for us. Monk followed her to the on-deck circle.

Coach wasn't finished. "Pitching strikes shows you off but also wears you out. You'll throw fewer times if you let your fielders work. Stop trying to make those Prince William fellows miss every ball. Make them hit it on your first pitch. Or second. Hit grounders. Pop-ups. Junk hits that your infielders handle."

Under his breath Randy said, "Pitching's the name of the game."

"Make no mistake—you'll feel it," Coach told him. "Fourth inning, fifth inning. Your arm will go. You'll give up extra-base hits to their weakest players."

Randy didn't hang his head the way DumDum always would when Coach corrected him. He didn't say, "Yes, sir" like Monk. He prowled the dugout, wanting to pitch more. He hadn't even put on his jacket to keep his arm warm. He searched the home-plate screen. He said, "Coach, the same pro scout as last year is there looking me over. They judge on strikes."

Coach sat fast. Everyone else in the dugout strained to glimpse a real big-league scout. I saw nothing unusual through the wire behind home plate, only outlines of Ronald Mergler, Jr., and Arthur Rinehart. My pal put film in his camera. Mr. Mergler wrote in his notebook. What else is new? I swung my Louisville Slugger on my way to the on-deck circle.

We hadn't scored in our half of the first inning, but we weren't out yet. Aileen had bunted safely and darted to third on Monk's single. Ben lined out to the shortstop. DumDum swung hard three times and missed. Eugene got nicked by a pitch and didn't try to nick back. He held first base, not kicking the bag or himself. In the box, E.J. balanced her bat lightly above her right shoulder. She kept still—still—until the ball hit the outside corner as E.J. hit it. With a crack she was on her way to first and Aileen scooting home.

My turn at bat: first time: first season.

I settled my helmet. I cocked my Slugger. I waited to be lonely. Monk always says how lonely he feels in the batter's box with no one to help, just him against the enemy pitcher in a brutal duel. Something like that. I waited for Monk's feeling through

"Strike one."

I didn't get lonely. For helpers I had three runners on base, each watching me intently. E.J. smiled from first. Eugene shaded his eyes for a better view. Monk, with a small lead off third, called, "Bring me around—bring us all around, Zanner." Beyond him, in the dugout, the other Generals took up his call. "Getahit!" "Lookemover!" "Sucker!" Randy shouted to his opposing pitcher. Coach flashed me a signal from the top step: "Swing away," he said by brushing the letters across his chest. Jumbo Williams wasn't so subtle. "Cream it," I heard him holler all the way from our bull pen. "Sock it down their throats," every Lee High kid began to chant. Lurleen Dewey egged them on.

"Ball one."

Voices came from behind the screen. "Way to look." Sounded like Mr. Mergler. Another man's voice said, "Close call. The little lady's got nerves. Good eyesight. And she took the first pitch like Ted Williams always said." A chair creaked. A camera clicked.

How could a ball player be lonely in the batter's

54

box with all these friends around?

"Strike two."

Even my enemies kept me company. The umpire's decision seemed right in my ear. The Prince William catcher agreed. "Fooled ya, girlie," he said. He stood up and giggled. His shin guards clattered. He planted his mitt for the next pitch. I felt his breath on my back. I felt his mitt near my hip. I didn't feel lonely.

"Ball two."

Jeers from the Princes' bench jockeys cheered me up, not down. I almost laughed. I knew I wasn't a "turkey." Prince substitutes booed and bellowed in chorus: "Pressure—pressure, meathead. You're gonna strike out." I didn't feel I would. I felt cozy waiting there.

"Ball three."

Teammates leading off bases. Friends screaming from bleachers. My coach flashing the same sign now, four pitches later. Their coach calling, "Come on, come on. We don't have all day." But I wanted all day. I wanted this at bat to last forever with its sights and tastes and feelings. The bed-sheet banner flapping over a railing. Rinehart's gumdrop under my tongue. The umpire's broom against my shoe. I wanted the sounds to last. . . . Rinehart's voice when their pitcher stretched for his sixth pitch to me: "Hit this, Zanboomer," my pal yipped from close behind me.

With that, the ball was gonners.

I boomed it over the fence and under a school bus. I ran the bases with an eye on that scout. I didn't run fast. No need. I didn't slide home. I bounced in to meet the outstretched hands of runners scoring ahead of me. Monk's hug. Eugene's handshake. E.J.'s tap on my batter's helmet. All our runs put us Generals ahead in this game for good.

Two hours later we left Lee Stadium with a winning streak of 1.

Chapter 7

And 2. We clobbered Front Royal in our second exhibition game.

On the team bus riding down there, Randy read us his fan mail. He'd brought it along in stacks wrapped with rubber bands. Every page he'd smooth on top of his Adidas bag. He'd shout, "Feast on this, you-all." He'd pronounce the dates first. "April 5; April 7; April 10, that's yesterday. A girl left a love letter with my homeroom teacher. Hey, there's no date on this, but listen up to what Tammy Pam Tupper says."

Dearest Superarm!
    You are my sports hero!
    I love how your uniform keeps clean all game long!
    Please send me a piece of your shirt to keep beside my picture of you from the *Herald*!
    Good luck forever!

                       xxxxoooo

Fritz snorted. "Heckuva letter from a nine-year-old kid."

"Yep, she's my girl friend's little sister," DumDum woke up to say. "Are we there yet?"

We stayed loose on the bus, kidding Randy about his feeble-minded fans. Coming home to Arlington, we were even looser because we'd won by nine runs. We recited our batting averages. We ate hot dogs that Mr. Mergler passed out as he went up and down the aisle holding interviews. Even Eugene nibbled the meat part, telling why he was changed to number five in our batting order. "Coach knows I have my slumps and ups. He also knows I'm working hard on my weight problem. I'd rot first before I'd bat ninth." Eugene remembered calories and handed DumDum his catsupy bun.

Mr. Mergler asked E.J. about Randy, how she liked playing on the same team with such a showboat. "He's not," she said in her soft voice. "For example, his big kick and prolonged follow-through—they prove his love for pitching, not that he's showing off." Mr. Mergler turned around and asked Randy about E.J., maybe to start up some controversy. Randy surprised us. He folded his fan letters and said, "Eleanor Johnston would help any team in our league just by riding a bus with them. Look how she calms us. She gives the Generals class."

"And you, Walter. Did any of the pitches you hit come through the strike zone?" Mr. Mergler's pen moved swiftly.

DumDum couldn't answer. He'd fallen asleep, his head against the window. Monk acted as spokesman. He reviewed the fifth inning, Aileen's defensive "gem" of a throw and DumDum's triple that sounded like a van hitting a stop sign. Monk described his own injury. "I twisted my knee in the fifth breaking up a double play at second base. But I'll be one hundred percent prepared for our

58

Northern Division debut in a week."

"Me too," I said, half awake. Other questions sounded simple. "Is Michael O'Hara the best coach in Virginia?" In the world, I thought. "Is Ben Brown afraid of the curve?" If he is, we love him anyway. "Will Zan's base running catch up with her hitting and throwing?" Who needs running? I went to sleep on Monk's shoulder.

We took up tons of space in the *Herald* sports page because of our winning streak. After we closed the exhibition season by bumping off D.C. Memorial, we played league teams, three a week. Randy and Jumbo rotated pitching. Jumbo gave up a few runs in his games, but we always scored them back. And more: Lee Generals 8, Alexandria Eagles 4; Lee 6, Fairfax 2. With Randy on the mound, us fielders almost didn't need our gloves. He threw strikes and shutouts: Lee 5, Quantico Lutheran 0; Lee 3, Friends Academy 0. Over the regular season we'd meet every team in our division twice. Also the Redskins—from the Southern Division—once.

Every week got more fun. We sang on the bus to our first night game and joked about bashing homers to the moon. We warmed up casually on Swanson's new field, which seemed more like a garden than a place to slug baseballs. The grass was just cut. It smelled sweet, along with the candy apples in the stands. The bags, the lines had been coated with fresh white lime. They sparkled under lights so strong I could see Coach's fungoes as well as in daytime. When I missed one, I'd laugh at my own mistake. Coach laughed and shouted our nicknames

59

we'd invented for each other. Eugene became "Meat." That's all we ever saw him eat. Monk was Monk because of his St. Christopher medal and how he crossed himself in the on-deck circle. E.J. stayed E.J. I turned into Boomer. Boomer Hagen. Rinehart said I earned it because of my batting average: .395.

After that game—Lee Generals 10, Swanson Admirals 0—we hung around our dugout, enjoying final chirps from Lurleen. Mr. Mergler asked his questions through a shower of popcorn tossed by majorettes. They'd forgotten confetti. They hadn't forgotten their batons, and I borrowed Ruby Jean's to show Mr. Mergler my swing up close. Buddy had stashed the bats until tomorrow's practice.

"Here's how I hit safely in the third inning," I said, swinging from my heels. I twisted around in a complete circle. "I timed one of Vanderkallen's fastballs right."

"You're a natural, Zanboomer."

"No she's not," Rinehart piped out. He sat on the dugout railing taking pictures for the *Herald*. "She's struggled heroically to be a boomer." His flashbulb went off in my face.

I said, "Lookit how natural I am." I tried to twirl the baton. It dropped. "I can't twirl naturally." Then I swung the baton from my regular stance. I kept swinging and talking. "Every day, all spring and summer for years, I've swung my same bat. At tennis balls. At rocks. At hard-boiled eggs and Dixie cups—any spheres my brother threw at me. Anything on my batting tee. I broke the neighbor's window with a peach pit. Nights I worked in front of a mirror. You call that natural? Practice! Coach has us in the batting cage until dark some days. Our team works like—"

"Beavers." Rinehart finished my sentence.

Mr. Mergler wrote down our tips. Next evening the *Herald* sports page printed these headlines.

HARD WORK IS SECRET
OF GENERALS' SUCCESS

Trounce Admirals for Eighth Straight
Two Games Away from May 1 Showdown with
Undefeated Redskins

That was better than Tammy Pam Tupper's letters. Most of us Generals had a stack from her by now. She changed her luck forevers, depending on how we scored the date she wrote. April 18, she asked Ben for an autographed picture. April 25, she begged Aileen for a souvenir curl. Me she told I could be her future favorite if only I didn't get caught in rundowns. She didn't sign that letter with hugs and kisses. I stored it in my locker anyway.

The locker room felt like a sports prom before our double header with St. Vincent's Prep. We shined our shoes and oiled our gloves. Buddy ironed our undershirts, calling them tuxedoes. We suited up in our home-game uniforms extra carefully, but right along we whistled Lee's fight song or hummed with

Jumbo's radio, which he turned up louder than usual. Eugene asked Fritz for a dance. They clomped around the bat bags in their spikes like a pair of pinstriped clowns. Ben asked Aileen. She wouldn't dance, for a change. She wouldn't unfrizz her hair with sweat until her boyfriend saw it on field. He played catcher for St. Vincent's Prep. Besides, she had 108 things to finish before our games. She polished her barrettes. She autographed a baseball for some kid in Arlington Hospital. She sprayed the air with perfume so we'd "smell like a clique." She answered fan mail on stationery that said: "Vote Aileen Dickerson Prom Queen." She arranged her towel a certain way none of us could figure out. It stood like a candle, ready for her shower after we won.

Buddy folded our clean towels in perfect squares and passed them out with Dentyne, as many sticks as we wanted. I already had a pocketful of Rinehart's gumdrops. And a shelfful of towels. But I asked for tape to cover a heel blister.

"Anything you suggest shall be yours," promised Buddy. "As long as we beat Joe Donn Joiner's gang next week."

"Anything? Okay, hamburgers, manager," Meat said.

"Please turn this machine off, Buddy," Monk called. Wrapped in a robe, he straddled the whirlpool. He'd soaked his leg in hot, churning water, but I could tell his knee still hurt. He winced a lot. He wouldn't dance with any of us. He'd save his speed for St. Vincent's. Dr. Ableson, our trainer, gave Monk the once-over, told him to wear a knee guard, and went to work on Randy's right arm. Massaging it. Pouring on alcohol. Getting it ready to pitch seven innings. Randy lay on the rubdown table saying, "Yeah, yeah, Doc." Jumbo danced a solo, awaiting his turn on the table.

Spikes and dancing and pinstripes and perfume— we had it all, seemed like. Plus DumDum sitting on his dressing stool reading aloud from his comic book. He made us laugh with his hammy southern accent. He pronounced the words in time to Jumbo's music. "A-Biff. A-Bash. A-Boom." He rolled up the comic and practiced swinging. "I might be hitterish today," he confided. "If St. Vincent's pitcher makes one wrong mistake—off the field with that ball." DumDum drank lemonade E.J.'s mom had made.

Who needed lemonade? Who needed gumdrops? We had each other for strength and refreshments.

You never saw such a team effort. We all felt hitterish. We knocked two pitchers out of the first game and the same two out of the second. DumDum's comic book came true. Biff—an infield single. Bash— a triple. Bam—a barrage of baseballs off our pet bats. We held a slugfest while the Lee band threw streamers of blue crepe paper and played the Lee hymn on kazoos. "Gimme a Z for Zanboomer." Our cheerleaders gave a hand-cupped holler. "Gimme M's for Monk and Meat," DeeDee called. "Bring on the Redskins." Our pom-pom girls continued the chant.

We deserved it. On field we robbed St. Vincent's of scores right and left. Monk played second like a demon, even with his knee practically in a sling. E.J. glided around as if she wore ice skates. Eugene wasn't a third baseman—he was an acrobat. He sprang and twisted and rolled and took a header one time, closing the gap in a rundown. Out in straight-away center field Ben chased a liner deeper than ever, locked his hand on the chain fence, and vaulted in the air. His glove must have been nine feet high full of baseball. After that third out in the seventh inning, Jumbo stood stunned on the mound. He waited for Ben to come by on his way off field. Jumbo put his arm over Ben's shoulder as they walked to our dugout.

We belonged there together. We all piled up our hands and cheered ourselves. "Gimme a T for team-mates," I said in our perfumy huddle.

"Bring on the Redskins."

Bring on Joe Donn Joiner.

Chapter 8

FIRST INNING

Here comes Joe Donn Joiner to the Redskin mound.

Richmond Stadium echoes with approval.

Joe Donn's a hero of three sports per year.

He's six feet tall.

The mound is fifteen inches high.

That makes Joe Donn seven feet three inches.

He doesn't look so mean today.

Not as bad as in his red football face mask.

Not as up close as in basketball games.

He's sixty feet six inches away from our batters.

From there he strikes out the side.

SECOND INNING

For openers, Joe Donn shouts, "Hey, DumDum, you mental midget, don't crowd the plate or I'll brain ya." DumDum hops on home plate. He points to the Redskin pennant they won last year in the Virginia State Series. It's blowing in a stiff wind out over a left-field billboard that's supposed to be a fence. DumDum tells Joe Donn, "Put your first pitch anywhere near me—I'll knock it out there."

Joe Donn does and DumDum does.

Score: 1–0, Generals.

Eugene steps up. All weekend before this game he's been even-tempered: mad. His dark features are set in a glower. He swings and misses, swings and misses. Then PSHEWW. He connects. Halfway down to first, Eugene sees the ball bouncing into the bull pen for a ground-rule double. He stops sprinting and starts skipping and clapping all the way to second.

He dies there. E.J. pops foul to their catcher, Dwayne Yelverton. He flips off his catcher's mask to make the play. From where I kneel in the on-deck circle Dwayne looks mean as Joe Donn. He calls, "I got it, chump" to E.J.

Next up, I swing, swing. Crack. I hit a broken-bat bouncer across their pebbly infield. I don't beat the throw from shortstop. I walk back to the dugout and mourn my pet bat.

Fritz is still swinging at strike three after the ball is tucked safely in Dwayne's mitt.

We strand Eugene. He's madder.

THIRD INNING

The Redskin bench jockeys taunt us because we're shutting them out, 1–0. They try to ruin our concentration on field. They try to give Randy the shakes. Already we're thinking about the raw, windy day. Rotten weather for a vital game. We want to flop in our dugout, away from dust swirling around the diamond, stinging our eyes. I flump my bare hand against my gloved hand to keep them both warm. The razzing gets noisier.

"Hey, DumDum, you're the league's most valuable player."

"Yea, from the neck down."

"Who's that whale belly playing third?"

"Aw, Ump, their pitcher's throwing spitters."

"There goes your no-hitter, Boyle."

True. Dwayne Yelverton singles from his threatening stance. And the second guy up lines a pitch six inches over Eugene's cap. Dwayne rockets past second and into third without sliding. He stands tall on the bag. Not as tall as Eugene, who glares at him. In the batter's box, Joe Donn sweeps his hand the full length of his bat. He's ready to paste his rival's pitch. He goes down on one knee in a vicious cut at a curve. He check swings at ball three. His teammates on the bench growl their help. They bombard Randy with useless advice.

"Hey, Boyle, you're falling apart."

"Throw your spitball, wetfingers, so the ump can kick you out of the game."

"Hey, pitcher man, you better hit Joe Donn in his pitching arm or he'll beat you today."

Fritz calls time out. He jogs halfway to the mound. "C'mon, Pro, make 'em hit." Randy nods to a row of scouts huddled under jackets and coats. They puff cigars. The smoke floats to where I wait to help Randy. Fritz looks to Coach O'Hara for a sign. It's "Make him hit."

Our infield sets for the double play. Fritz offers his mitt for a target. Randy winds up. He drives toward the plate in his usual rhythm. He strikes out Joe Donn. We hold our infield positions. Randy strikes out the Redskins' number one and number two batters. We race to our dugout under a hail of peanut shells heaved by angry Redskin rooters. Randy doesn't race. He walks slowly from the mound. He's getting tired.

FOURTH INNING

	1	2	3	4	5	6	7		R	H	E
GENERALS	0	1	0	0					1	1	0
REDSKINS	0	0	0	0					0	2	0

FIFTH INNING

Randy's in trouble.

He's taking longer between pitches. He keeps on shaking his arm as if he has a kink in it. He picks up the rosin bag oftener. He throws to first base more, holding the Redskin runner close. He bluffs throws to third, his eye on that runner. Randy rubs up the new ball he asks for. Finally he stretches. He throws ball three to Rex DeLeo, who leads his league in home runs. Rex backs out of the box, stoops, and pours dust from hand to hand.

Randy turns around to check his outfielders' positions. He waves Ben deeper into center. He waves Aileen farther to the left. The new ball must not feel perfect because he asks for another. Fritz scrubs it against his chest protector, taking the shine off. Monk hurries to the mound to wipe the ball hard against his knee brace. They both stir up dust with their spikes.

Randy's having trouble with his footing. He almost flings himself from the mound pitching ball four to Rex.

Now, with one out and Redskins leading off every base, Randy faces their cleanup man. He works slower than ever. After ball two he shouts to the umpire: "Hey, Umpire, who taught you to call pitches? Helen Keller?" He thumbs his nose in disgust.

The umpire ignores Randy.

The batter doesn't. He swings and misses Randy's third pitch. He examines his bat in wonder. He tells the umpire, "I think Boyle threw me a spitter." Missing a shoulder-high pitch, he gripes, "I know that was a spitball—I could smell Dentyne on it."

"Time out!" The umpire demands to inspect the ball for wetness. Randy says, "Sure," and rolls it sixty feet to home plate. Evidence dries in the dust.

But Randy's still in trouble.

His flowing motions are gone. His cap's awry. The name on his uniform is soaked with sweat even this cold day. No longer is he pitching his pro style, as if watching himself in a mirror. He walks home a run to tie the game, 1–1.

Redskin bench jockeys suddenly love him. They smack their lips in fake kisses. "Yoo-hoo—Boyle, there goes your shutout," they holler. Coach O'Hara stalks to the mound through a snowstorm of trash from standees. He signals Jumbo Williams to hurry warming up. He quietly asks Randy what's the matter. I hear the question. I'm there in the huddle with Fritz and Monk and our worn-out pitcher.

"Coach, I'm losing my stuff. My curve won't break big. I can't throw hard with control."

"Your own fault. You've already thrown one hundred and twenty-three times in only five innings. I hope those scouts have seen enough. I can't pamper you. You're gone." Coach takes the ball from Randy, who ducks his head and bolts for the dugout.

"Heckuva game," Fritz calls after him. Monk and I agree by clapping, but the Redskinettes drown us out with boos for our first-string pitcher.

We wait on the mound for Jumbo's amble in from the bull pen. He pulls his spikes through the outfield weeds to clean them off. He bends to touch second base for good luck. He unzips his warm-up jacket and exchanges it for the ball. "The Redskins weren't hitting Randy," Jumbo says. Coach comes back with "Randy wasn't getting them out this inning, either. You must coax them to hit to your infield. Keep the ball down and on the inside corner to this next batter. He hammered a high inside fastball last year in the series for a triple." Coach strides away saying, "Let's get them out."

"Hey, let's be winners. There's nothing like it." Monk encourages our fielders to start up action again.

All us Generals are soon in heavy trouble. With one out, bases loaded, the batter sets up quickly, eager to test Jumbo's arm. He smithereens the first pitch over DumDum's head in right field. DumDum chases that hit to the billboard fence. He picks it up and fires a bullet—but to first base, the wrong base. Every Redskin has scored except one diving for third. What good can E.J. do with the ball? Stay cool, is what. By a snap of her slender wrist she hits Eugene's glove. He tags the runner who's been trying to stretch a double into a triple. Eugene and the ex-runner scuffle until the third-base umpire pulls them apart. Redskins stream out of their dugout, ripe for a fight. We hold our positions instead.

Our game is untied: Redskins 4, Generals 1. Jumbo gets the next batter to slam a line drive directly at my forehead. I use my arm in self-defense. The ball nearly tears my hand off. "Hold on, hold on," I say to my trusty glove. The fifth inning's over when I do.

TOP HALF, SIXTH INNING

Our dugout at Richmond Stadium feels musty and unhomey. The water cooler smells moldy. Splintery benches are sunk low in the ground. Our spirits sink lower. Monk seems close to tears with his hurt knee and zero runs today. Aileen's eyelashes drip mascara on the bat rack, where she's leaning her face away from us. Fritz cusses at a broken strap on his leg guard. Overhead, our tin roof catches soda cans hurled by the Redskin mob. They're reminding us of their lead.

Our first batter, Ben, strikes out on five curves.

Coach O'Hara keeps telling Randy to go take a shower, but Randy wants to see the rest of our game. Eugene mutters, "What rest? Oh, you mean when we rot."

Randy says, "Don't be too sure. Joe Donn's thrown almost as many times as I did. He's been sneaking

71

looks at the scouts. He's bushed, too."

Not all that much. Our second batter, DumDum, strikes out on nine pitches.

Before Eugene leaves the dugout, Coach asks him what kind of pitch he doubled in the second inning. Eugene remembers a high fastball. Coach asks him what kinds of pitches struck him out in the fourth. Eugene remembers sliders and one knuckleball.

Randy says, "Joe Donn isn't throwing anything but fastballs and curves this inning. He's lost control of his other stuff. Wait for *your* pitch. Swing like before."

"Do it, Meat."

"Youkindoitagain, baby."

Eugene watches call strike one, two. He clubs home plate in frustration. He doesn't watch another. In comes Joe Donn's high fastball. Out it sails to our empty bull pen. "That woulda killed you, Jumbo," Fritz warns with a grin. "Lucky you're safe underground with us."

E.J.'s up there now. That means I'm due in the on-deck circle. But I can't decide on a bat. My favorite's broken, and Ben's that I borrowed in the fourth inning's too light. I heft every bat on the rack. I notice colors. I don't like maroon. I don't like aluminum ones. They sound funny. I read the printing on a thirty-two ounce wood Wilson. I read the fine print: "Power-fused Northern White Ash." It matches my dusty shoes. I read the signature: Henry Aaron.

While I'm reading, E.J. gets hit by a Joe Donn curve. All our guys jump up with their fists tight. "Didja see that?" Fritz eggs them on.

"Sure," says Randy. "She hung there and took it. That's class when we need it. Joe Donn's losing his curve. Zan, you'll see fastballs from him."

Fast. Curves. Same difference if I don't choose the right bat. DumDum gives me his. "It made a homer in the second," he tells me.

I lug his heavy bat to the on-deck circle. I cover the handle with pine tar. I'm already thinking I better bunt. A bat's easier to control on a bunt. Say I see a fastball down the middle. I'll surprise Joe Donn. I'll surprise myself if I beat the throw. I take a slugging stance. I circle my head with the bat and uncrook my neck. I'll trick Joe Donn into thinking—

I face him and point to the pennant beyond left field. I call, "You, pitcher! This bat I'm swishing belongs to Walter Cadden. You've already seen how not dumb he is. Also, his signature's here on the fat end." I tap the fat on home plate. "Put your first pitch anywhere near me—I'll put it next to his."

Joe Donn shouts, "No way you can. Nohow. Nowhere."

I toss my totally straight hair the way Aileen does her curls. I hang poised the way E.J. does.

Joe Donn's fastball flies in at me slow.

And I won't ever know if I could have beaten his throw to first. He never throws to first! He can't believe my bunt. It trickles toward him on the pocky field. The bat is out of my hands before I've counted two steps. Ten steps later, Joe Donn's still on the mound, a seven-foot statue. His catcher yells, "It's yours." His first baseman yells, "It's yours." Someone else yells, "It's mine." Sounds like Eugene, who must be to third base because I'm safe across first after twenty-two steps.

I whirl to see what's happening. The statue blinks down at my dusty bunt. To him it's a stink bomb. He reaches for it with his big pitcher's glove. He twists to find me at first. He narrows his eyes savagely and moves them to second. E.J. leans off base. Nothing in her peaceful face shows she plans to budge. She budges when Joe Donn throws home, trying to snuff out Eugene. Eugene doesn't beat the throw, so he hits Yelverton hard and high. Dwayne ooooofs over backwards. He tags air with his bare hand. Somewhere under two bodies is the baseball. E.J. takes third. I take second. We both rip home on Fritz's single.

Our dugout's still dank, but more from torrents of nervous sweat than from cold concrete. Plus the water cooler leaks. Eugene kicked it in happiness over our 4–4 tie. He hugs my bat with the same force he used on Yelverton. He can't stop hugging it. "Dynamite bunt. You tricked Joe Donn," he shouts to the tin roof. Ben tells me I'm catching up to my friend Rinehart. "You schemed your way on," he says.

I pose like a hero. "After we win, just set me down easy, in case you carry me off the field," I declare to our bench.

"Pipe down, everyone. No more shenanigans, Matello." Coach O'Hara knows we aren't ahead. "Let's not swing and hope," he calls to Jumbo at the plate. Coach climbs three steps and gives the sign to hit and run. He signals Aileen to go into her on-deck act, to wear Joe Donn out even more.

Jumbo pretends not to hear the rackety Redskin crowd. He waits with his bat nailed to his shoulder. Every pitch to him is a ball way outside, four of them for an intentional walk. He lumbers to first.

"If Joiner prefers to work on Aileen, so be it," Coach says.

"Sucker," Randy can't help yelling.

Aileen pretends not to feel the chilly wind blowing her pants against her legs. She plucks up her sleeves. They puff sideways. She jangles her bracelets until Dwayne Yelverton squints behind his mask and asks the umpire to make her stop. Joe Donn gets even by twirling his Virginia State Series game ring around in plain sight on his finger. He's rattled anyway. He serves up unintentional ball four. Aileen zips to first.

Where she doesn't dance off because the ground is mushy there, only spot on the diamond. The Redskins watered first base to stop her from taking that extra jump. They've heard she leads the league in stealing. She shakes her bracelets at Monk, urging him to bring the runners home.

Monk's up. And he swings from the waist up. His legs don't stride. One's stiff. One hurts. He slashes at the ball with anxious strokes. He misses. He seems lonelier than ever in the box. He's lost his groove because of injuries. He decides to let Joe Donn walk him in. He looks at the third strike. Monk's out.

Side retired.

Generals 4, Redskins 4.

"Joiner's not dead yet," Coach cautions. Before we leave for the field he reminds us how to set up for the next Redskin batters. "Shortstop deep for

Yelverton. Hagen, your arm can make up the distance. Matello—that fellow who hit over your head—move back on him and closer to the foul line. Tell Dickerson to shade him left—shallow left. When Joiner bats, everybody awake. He'll be up to something. Alert Jumbo that once he cuts the ball loose he's an infielder, not a pitcher. He must not watch what happens. I want him to come off the mound and play defense."

We empty the bench with Coach's warnings in our ears. Shadows fall over Richmond Stadium. The pale sun gives up and fades behind outfield billboards.

BOTTOM HALF, SIXTH INNING

Dwayne Yelverton fires a cannon shot at me. I snare it in the top of my glove webbing. One out.

Aileen buzzes ten yards, then dives headlong for Laddie Griffen's sinking liner. She's lost in dust and shadows, making out two.

We're following our game plan. Goose eggs for the Redskins now.

Jumbo pumps, kicks, strides, releases, follows through—stays on the mound while Joe Donn's boomer climbs steeply and vanishes. Joe Donn runs low to the ground. He stabs each canvas bag with both feet. He passes me snarling, "For you, Zanbunter—my fartherest homer."

"I can do that," I say back to bluff him. I can't think of whether to smile. My head is worrying about the next inning, our last at bat. Like a spectator I watch another homer and then Monk hobble toward a grounder. He gloves the ball and throws for the inning-ending out. Redskins 6, Generals 4.

FINAL INNING

Click.
Click.
Click.
My spikes take our dugout steps one at a time, careful not to slip on damp concrete. No point breaking a leg until after the series in June. We'll have our next chance then to beat the 'Skins, if we both win our division races.

Randy greets us with a chart he's been keeping of Joe Donn's pitches. He reviews the numbers with Ben and DumDum before their final trips to the plate. "Joe Donn's slider's gone, his fastball. He's throwing nothing but off-speed stuff now. No smoke. He's changed his motion. Look at him warm up! He's pretending to put extra effort into his delivery. Wind up faster. But see how he breaks his leg against the mound and doesn't dive out of his crouch?"

Joe Donn's pitches pass through the strike zone slow. His turn up, Ben redirects one into center field and skids to second base on DeLeo's error. DumDum cracks a single. Ben rounds third. He turns back, afraid he might be cut down at home. He's not speedy like Aileen. He's smart, though. He checks Coach for a signal. Coach is busy sending Eugene to bat. With advice and a soothing pat, Eugene steps in to aim for the bull pen again. This time his hit soars high in the heavy air. It hangs long enough for Laddie Griffen's breadbasket catch. Ben tags up and scores. DumDum holds first. Eugene comes back to our dugout and stomps so hard on his batter's helmet that he can't pull it off his spikes. I don't have a minute to help him. I'm finding a bat ... I'm warming the skinny handle . . . I'm swinging all the way on deck. . . .

How can I be up again?

Here's how. I'm number seven batter and E.J. just struck out. I guess at summer camp she didn't practice on slow pitches. DumDum's still over there on first. Two outs. Last inning. They're ahead, 6–5. I'm up for sure in the darkening stadium.

Up without a trick. Joe Donn's got his mean narrow eyes on me. Ditto Dwayne Yelverton. I feel them piercing my legs as he squats his masked self over the plate.

Where's Rinehart now that I need a scheme worse than ever?

DumDum's bat weighs around a thousand pounds.

What's the sign from Coach? He's brushing the letters across his chest. He's stopping at letter R. Swing away and run for your life. Good thinking, Coach. My bat's too heavy to whip. The ball inches in from a background of clouds. I see my baseball life spiraling toward me. Billions of hits. Hits off a batting tee, hits in alleys, driveways, backyards. Hits through neighbors' windows. I'm six years old, cocking a plastic bat. I'm eight, wearing my brother's cleats and waving his too-long bat. I'm eleven, booming a softball across the girls' field onto Lee High track. I'm now, a mate with the whole Generals team calling

78

my name: "Zanboomer! Zanboomer!" Keep our rally alive is what they mean.

I do. Joe Donn's pitch is low and wide. I choke DumDum's bat. I poke the baseball toward a neighbor's window, one hundred miles away in Arlington. Who knows where the ball really lands in that dark outfield of rocks and weeds and Redskins. I don't look. I can't hear anything except my own shoes running, my own mind saying, "Faster. Faster." My feet listen. No one tags me at first. I round the bag and its Redskin defender. DumDum's not ahead. Second base is empty. "Run there," I tell myself, watching Rex DeLeo and Laddie converge on my hit ricocheting off a billboard.

"Go! Go!" A voice breaks through my own thoughts. Coach? Rinehart? Against the background of bleacher screams I can't tell. Touching second, I wonder if the voice means me. I'd better run to make sure. Third base and safety wait ninety feet down this white line.

"GOGOGO!" Coach O'Hara means me. He's behind third in the box, waving me on. No time for fancier signals. "Keep running," he yells at me.

I look to see what's next. DumDum's safe at home because someone overthrew Dwayne Yelverton. Dwayne's mask is off. He's pedaling backwards to snatch the ball. He's groping around. He's shouting for Joe Donn to cover the plate.

"Get her. Get her." Joe Donn leaves his mound as I race down the third-base path. We're both sixty feet from Yelverton's throw. Clomp, clomp, clomp, clomp. I've stopped counting my heavy footsteps. Joe

Donn's faster than me. He's already there. I try to fight him off with my eyes. Yelverton stands next to him at home plate.

Some home!

"Gotcha!"

Dwayne's arm comes toward me on a deadly line. I hook-slide away from the bag. He finds me with an ax stroke. He doesn't keel over backwards. He falls forward on me. My right arm twists beneath him. I'm pinned with my teeth in his chest protector.

"Safe."

Safe but not safe. Suddenly another body grinds me farther into the ground. Pain spreads from shoulder to elbow. My whole arm's studded with pain. I laugh kind of, cry kind of, while above me every baseball player in the world seems to be battering another. I ask someone, "Don't move my arm. Pick me up easy."

"That's taps."

"Help her, someone."

The playing field tips out from under me.

Chapter 9

ZANBOOMER SLIDES
ALL THE WAY TO
ARLINGTON HOSPITAL

Lee Shortstop Mauled at Richmond Plate
Teams Erupt in Game-Ending Brawl

BY RONALD MERGLER, JR.

Special to the *Herald*
ARLINGTON, Virginia, May 2—The Robert E. Lee Generals and the Richmond Redskins, two dominant teams in Virginia school baseball and perennial rivals, met yesterday at the capital's decrepit stadium. Their showdown turned into a shoot-out that left several players injured, one of them seriously. Lee's rookie shortstop, Suzanne "Zanboomer" Hagen, was removed by ambulance to Richmond Civic Hospital, X-rayed, and transferred to Arlington County Hospital this morning. Contacted at home by telephone, the Generals' team physician reported that Hagen is under observation for a "possible concussion." She is also being treated for a shoulder injury of an "indeterminate nature."

In a contest marred by brush-back pitches, bruising tags, gibes from each bench, and an unruly home crowd hurling leftovers from the numerous food concessions, Hagen had little chance of surviving her seventh-inning slide into catcher Dwayne Yelverton *and* pitcher Joe Donn Joiner of the Redskins. She rose from the dust on a stretcher carried by opposing coaches, who were still yelling at each other long after their game had been suspended by a harried chief umpire and his associates.

Specific events preceding her injury and the slugfest are these: (1) with the Redskins leading, 6–5, with 2 outs and Walter Cadden on first base, Hagen slammed her patented "boomer" to right center field; (2) the ball fell between defenders Rex DeLeo and Laddie Griffen and caromed off the rickety billboard that serves as a fence; (3) after several tries by Griffen, DeLeo made the pickup and threw to his cutoff man at second base; (4) who tripped on the bag, throwing wild in an attempt to gun down slow-footed Cadden at home plate; (5) Cadden scored easily. Hagen—the possible winning run—rounded third on signal from Generals Coach Michael O'Hara.

From that moment it was a three-way race unlike any this reporter has seen in Virginia League action. As catcher Yelverton retrieved the overthrow, he urged his pitcher to cover home plate. Joiner outran Hagen, but by then Yelverton, perhaps remembering a sixth-inning fielding error by Joiner, had decided on an unassisted putout. He also beat Hagen home, yet she challenged him with such grit and accurate body placement that Yelverton dropped the ball. (He had done so earlier on General Eugene Matello's slide. It should be noted that Yelverton is rather small for a catcher.) Yelverton's next move seemed instinctive. He dumped himself on Hagen. Further, the umpire's "safe" call enraged bystanding Joiner. In his football style of piling on, he added himself to the mélange. Within seconds, Generals poured on field; and, delighting hometown fans, fistfights broke out around the fallen body of Zanboomer.

Umpires sought to quash the fracas quickly, but it worsened until assistance from groundsmen, ushers, and finally ambulance attendants was needed to subdue most players. (Curiously, the fabled Fighting Eugene Matello failed to appear in this "main event." Interviewed later, he revealed that he had been unable to run or walk from the dugout because of a batting helmet stuck to both shoes.) The game could not be concluded because of darkness. Umpires disagreed among themselves as to a fair settlement. Coaches and school officials protested possible "endings"; and the final decision, reached after midnight by Virginia League Commissioner Dillard Jefferson, is that later this season the teams will resume playing at the exact point their game ended—Redskins 6, Generals 7 on Hagen's 2-run boom.

Their bus ride home proved a sorrowful journey for the Generals. Despite boasts of fisticuff heroics and a moral victory in Richmond, players seemed most deeply concerned with the severity of Hagen's injuries. Conversation centered on the team's plight if Hagen is lost for this year. According to O'Hara, her "hustle, alertness, big bat, and strong arm will be irreplaceable," thus weakening his chances for another title. Infielder Monk Cunningham speculated that "Zanboomer would miss the team more than it would miss her, if that's possible. Her whole life is sports." Schoolboy photographer Arthur Rinehart agreed. "She *is* her arm," he said of his long-time friend.

(Ed. Note: For Rinehart's photographs of game highlights, see page B12.)

Chapter 10

"Rinehart, I hate flowers."

"They cover up medicine smells."

"I hate get-well cards."

"Even this one from Tammy Pam?" Rinehart held up a cardboard baseball he found in the pile. "Shall I read you her poem, 'Boomer at the Bat'?"

"Later, maybe. I hate hospital lunches. They're gray and greasy."

"Don't touch that. Eat wheat-germ newtons and a handful of gumdrops I brought you."

His gifts stuck my teeth together, as usual. Rinehart continued reading cards from my teammates and friends and people I didn't even know. When he stopped I said, "I hate Dr. Ableson. This morning he mumbled every answer about my dumb arm. He spoke Latin, can you believe it? He said, 'acromioclavicular separation' when I asked. He won't look me in the eye. He wouldn't tell me when I can throw hard again. Or when I'll quit hurting. He wormed out of here before breakfast came."

"He means well."

If Rinehart says that, I know I'm in big trouble. It's his absolute worst criticism of someone. So I asked him, "Will you find out from Dr. Ableson when he's letting me escape this place? I'm due at practice. We play the Warriors Friday and the Admirals Saturday."

Rinehart ignored me. He read get-well cards in his chipperest voice. He pointed out the funny parts. He made me pay attention to the animals and what they said. He praised a homemade maroon card from Lurleen where in a poem she rhymed "slide" with "bride." On Ruby Jean's he showed me how the sequins sparkled under my bed lamp. On Fuzzy's card he asked me to count spelling errors. He straightened my blanket and laid out a row of cards for a contest. "We'll judge on the sentiment, not the art," he announced, covering my entire bed except where I had my sore arm in a sling. "Here's a card without a name," he noticed. "No initial, no return address, nothing except someone's printed 'Eat your heart out.'" Rinehart almost bit his tongue after he read that aloud. He scrutinized the envelope. "Postmarked Richmond. Must be Joiner." Rinehart looked sick and mad at the same time. "We won't enter his card in our contest."

After Randy Boyle's card won because he said he'd get Joe Donn back for me, Rinehart judged the flower arrangements. He liked ferns best. He didn't like violets because they'd died already. I awarded a booby prize to every vase of roses. Also to the nurse when she told Rinehart he should leave. As soon as she had given me a pill, Rinehart crept back to my bedside from the hospital library. He read me to sleep from his medical book. Better than a pill any day.

During evening visiting hours the whole Generals team came in their best clothes. I hardly recognized

DumDum wearing a bow tie, black eye, and gloomy expression. "I dunno. I thought it was curtains when they put you on the stretcher," he said. Monk didn't wear his baseball cap. I recognized his limp. "At least I'm not as bad off as you," he said for good cheer. Aileen had a cut lip from the fight, but she'd curled her hair same as for games. She sat on my bed and reported the latest events in her queen campaign. She described the dress she planned to wear at her coronation. I gave her my roses for a wrist corsage. Ben pinned my cards to the curtains, all but Joe Donn's. He passed it around the room until Fritz boasted, "We'll do a job on Joiner in the series."

"I'll flatten him then myself," I said.

"Yeah," said Eugene. He seemed ready to demolish my ice pitcher, but before he could go on a binge the nurse drove everyone away.

"Take care," E.J. whispered.

"I miss you behind me, saving grounders from going through," said Randy. "This week at practice I'm letting our guys hit to the infield. Your substitute's fingers are made of stone."

Monk left last. "We need your hits at practice, Zanboomer. Coach plans moving you up to second in the batting order until I'm out of my slump."

"See ya."

Pills put me to sleep. Nurses woke me up for a day after that. Other pills dulled my arm pain. My mom brought cupcakes to go with the hospital food. My dad brought Baby Ruth bars as a joke. My brother bought me a new bat, exact same as the one I'd broken in our Redskin game. I kept it with my glove between ridges in the blanket. I couldn't swing it to test the weight. My right arm hurt too much, even with pills. I could oil my glove with one hand. I could eat with one hand. I opened envelopes with my teeth and one hand.

Rinehart forged himself out of school all Thursday long. He sat beside my bed and read to me, when I let him, from a huge book called *Gray's Anatomy*. It sounded like Dr. Ableson. It sounded like it went on forever. It felt heavy enough for a five years' supply of book reports when Rinehart lifted it onto my blanket so I could see the pictures. "Don't bounce the bed. Don't bounce my arm, it hurts."

"Sorry. Can you see from there?"

I could see but I didn't want to. The words didn't make sense. *Deltoid. Pectoralis major. Serratus magnus. Trapezius.* The drawings didn't seem to match my body. "Why is the cover of the book green when it's called *Gray's Anatomy?*" I asked, to pretend I was looking.

"Gray wrote the book." Rinehart turned pages for me. "You can use it for Fuzzy's report this month."

"I'm reporting on *Play Winning Baseball.* Hand it here. I want to show you the very slide I put on Dwayne Yelverton in the seventh."

"You wrote *last* year's report on *Play Winning Baseball.* Besides, Gray will help you understand your own injury." Rinehart wouldn't lift the fifty-pound drawings from my blanket.

"Rinehart, I'm sleepy."

After that he got out his log and made a list of all my hits so far this season. He marked them on my new bat with his blackest pen: ~~卌~~ ~~卌~~ ~~卌~~ ~~卌~~ III. He figured out my fielding average: 1.000. That got me happy. He said I was faster each game on the base paths, according to his electric wristwatch, but not as fast as I should be to beat players like Joe Donn Joiner.

I knew that. I had lumps to prove it. When Rinehart left for lunch in the hospital cafeteria I tried to find pictures of legs. What's wrong with mine that makes them slower than Aileen's and Joe Donn's? Also, what's wrong with my arm? The doctors don't tell me, they ask me. Where does it hurt? Can you move this way? Can you flex it? Did the ice help? Does the heat help? For two straight mornings Dr. Ableson felt my shoulder and arm all up and down. He located "the center of pain," he said to the other doctor.

One good thing: My head doesn't ache. I can go back to school tomorrow with my arm in a tight sling, a special one with pads and buckles—more like a splint.

What I found out Friday morning in school is that slings aren't good for collecting autographs. Not like broken-arm casts. The kids in homeroom wanted to sign, but when they did they pressed against my arm. It hurt so much I gave up. Also, I gave up trying to cut my meat at our training table. Eugene took over with his big strong hands. He hacked steak the size of chocolate chips. For fun he mashed my peas into baby food He would have fed me except I didn't let him. I wasn't an invalid. I had a perfectly useful arm. "Maybe I can play today if I don't have to throw," I said as the team went to suit up for our home double-header with the Warriors. "I can catch one-handed," I bragged. I thumped my glove.

"Can you boom?" Fritz wanted to know.

"We'll need hits. Those Warriors lead the Northern Division in team batting average. According to Coach, they'll score their share today, even against me." Randy wasn't panicky. I guess at practice the team had laid game plans. I didn't know. I decided not to ask.

I stayed in the dugout and watched our first Warriors game next to Coach. He let me keep the chart on Randy. Together we noticed every kind of pitch thrown all seven innings. Randy wasn't depending on his strike-out balls as much as before. He used some other stuff to force outs to our fielders. Monk ran well on his stiff legs. My substitute at shortstop made one error. He also drove in a run. Generals 4, Warriors 2.

While the Generals played their second game of the doubleheader, I hid in the locker room. I straightened up my locker to give the substitute room for his gear. I threw away my *Herald* clippings taped all over the bulletin board. I took a steam bath that almost melted my sling. My hand poking out looked all shriveled and like the skin was peeling. Slings give you leprosy, I decided. When the team came in and dropped on their dressing stools, I knew they'd lost before Ben told me. Monk and Aileen cried. Jumbo stared into space. I called him over to the whirlpool and told him to soothe his worn-out arm. "Our first loss. I pitched awful. My fault," he told me.

"Mine," said Ben.

"Mine," said everyone.

Mine, I thought. How can I help with this sling around my neck? I jerked it. I tried to raise my arm a half inch. No, a tenth inch. Tears came to my eyes, it hurt so bad. Buddy helped me put my sweater around my shoulders. I gave up. I went into Coach's office and said, "Sir, feels like I'll miss tomorrow's rematch with the Admirals, but I know I'll be cured up for next week's games."

He moved his cap from where it lay on the visitors' chair. I sat down before he asked me to. He didn't give me the famous O'Hara glare. He looked away, like Dr. Ableson and Monk and Buddy and my father so far this week. He opened up with "These things take time. Your concussion was so slight you don't even have a headache today, do you?"

"No, sir."

"Your arm, well, that's a different matter. The full weight of two Richmond players—mmm—quite a shock. I should never have sent you home. I thought the ball had traveled farther past Yelverton. And he's so small for a catcher—so light—I didn't think— And I felt you could outrun Joe Donn Joiner." Coach rapped his knuckles on a typed paper. "This report on your arm from Dr. Ableson—mmm—the X rays show nothing broken. A fracture would knock you out for months. You'll be back . . ."

"When?"

Coach didn't know. Really, or he would tell me, I

suppose. My mom didn't know either. She drove me to the hospital Saturday morning for another bunch of X rays and a grilling. I had to hold a twenty-pound weight in my right hand.

"Please don't make me lift it." Pain shot from my shoulder to my fingertips.

"Get dressed, Miss Hagen." The doctor dictated notes to his nurse. They tightened the straps and buckles on my sling before Mom drove me back to school for the Admirals game.

This time Rinehart and I saw the action together from seats down the right-field line. A few fouls fell around us, and once Ben deliberately hit a liner that bounced off the low wall right in front of me. I hadn't brought my glove. I felt naked without it. I felt stupid in a sling, but I needed it. Every time someone in our row scrambled past me to go for a refreshment my arm got shoved. "Let me fasten it stiffer against your side," Rinehart advised when I groaned. "Let me help you."

And of course Rinehart helped me, as usual. He opened his briefcase and found me an aspirin. He brought me a Pepsi without jostling my arm. He kept my scorecard in his neatest scientific handwriting. He let me slap my one good hand against his back when I wanted to clap for my ex-teammates. He computed individual batting averages for the game when Monk tagged the last Admiral out at second base. Generals 5, Admirals 1. That got me happy.

Rinehart's wise idea was to hold our seats until the crowd went home. That way my arm would be safe from accidental bumps. We sat still five minutes before I had a better idea. "Let's go down on field and find out if I remember my positions for the league's best hitters," I said. "No one's around to start up another concussion contest."

The field had cleared fast of Admirals and Generals, of umpires, of everyone but grounds keepers. One raked the mound. Another hovered over home plate, laying down a wooden stencil to mark the batter's box for Monday's practice. I stayed out of their way in my shortstop position. I waited deep in the springy grass for a phantom line drive from Vanderkallen. I backed up deeper for a dream blooper. I stepped lightly on the infield topsoil. I could almost see a chopper high off the plate and over the pitcher's mound. I kept my right arm tight in the sling and trotted close to a groundkeeper.

"We finished dragging this infield, miss. We'd appreciate you'd save it for the Generals team."

I suppose he didn't recognize me out of uniform. And he's right: The field doesn't need scuffs from my hiking boots. I gave up. "Let's go, Rinehart."

Walking home, I felt angry and useless. I hadn't helped my team for almost a week. Who knows when I might be able to boom again. Even Rinehart couldn't promise me. He had no schemes right then for wrecked human bodies. Not saying a word, he puffed along beside me, swinging his log in his left hand and his briefcase with a healthy right arm. What's he doing with that arm, I wondered. He can't catch. He can't hit. Sadder than ever, I held my own

93

left arm against my right one. I put on some speed to sluff off my pal. I ran ahead of him. I gave up more.

From way down the street he called, "You still have your legs."

Chapter 11

He called again next morning, this time on the phone. No one but Rinehart would dare at 6 A.M. Sunday. Like once when his favorite blue racer snake croaked and he needed me to help with an autopsy.

I answered the phone, expecting another laboratory crisis. Maybe Rinehart's Mung spoiled. I wasn't sleeping anyway. I lay worrying about my arm all night.

"Are you awake? How's the old arm?"

"It hurts as bad as ever. What's happened in your basement, Dr. Rinehart?" Some scheme, sounds like.

"Only that I've been reading the Sunday *Herald* down there. Mr. Mergler mentions your name in his column. I'm bringing it over for your scrapbook."

As soon as Rinehart came I saw scheme in his eyes. Also, he carried a clipboard and stopwatch like Coach O'Hara. He wore a baseball cap and gym shoes. "You look weird in sneakers, Rinehart."

"You look silly in slippers. Put on your spikes. I'm taking you for a workout."

"But my dumb arm—"

"I'm working your legs, not your arm."

Good thing my spikes were upstairs under the bed. I'd cleaned them out of my locker to make way for the substitute. Rinehart laced and tied them for me as I read Mr. Mergler's sentence saying I might be out of the Generals' lineup another five weeks or more. "The guy's crazy," I told my pal. He agreed. He rooted through his briefcase and found me some photographs. He circled what I should study on them. He gave a single answer for my questions. "Legs."

"No, don't look at the arms. Look at the *legs.*"

His photographs were glossy enlargements of my last run scored—my slide against the Redskins. You could see Dwayne Yelverton hulking above me. You could see in the next picture how he fell across me. Crunch. I remembered hearing a pop in my shoulder. Then, in the third picture, Joe Donn jumped us both. His head turned away. I couldn't see if he smiled or what. In all three of Rinehart's enlargements a red Magic Marker circled my legs. Dwayne and Joe Donn never touched them. My legs kicked free. They floated free. They lay free.

"So what?"

"Well, as I said, you still have your legs. I plan to develop them until your arm recovers. You'll run faster than eight of your first-string teammates by the time you go into the lineup again."

"When?" All I cared about.

"Let's set a date together."

"This Wednesday for the Winchester game."

"I won't promise on arms. I'll promise to lengthen your stride. I'll keep the rest of you in condition while your arm heals."

That seemed smart. "You do good work," I said about Rinehart's pictures and his scheme.

We went outside in the warm May morning. Down

our driveway ran a grassy strip between two lanes of concrete. With his tape measure, Rinehart measured feet from Military Road to our garage. Eighty feet exactly. "If you start eight feet out on the road and run into the garage two feet, you'll have a ninety-foot base path, regulation length. Now examine these photographs with me."

Rinehart had taken movies of me running to first base in games. He'd counted steps same way I do sometimes if I'm legging out an important hit. He'd printed the film into huge blowups of my legs. He'd measured the length of each stride. "Your stride is too short," he complained to me. "Moving at top speed, excellent runners have strides that exceed their height. For instance, E.J. She's five feet nine inches, with a stride of five nine as she crosses the bag here." Rinehart put pictures of E.J. on top of me and my short stride. I understood what he meant by her stretched-out legs.

"She's faster than me," I admitted.

"She's faster partly because her stride is longer."

"She's taller than me—and her legs are longer. I see that." I tried to think up other excuses. "She's calmer. Her legs go to summer camp—"

"Yes, but look at Monk here. You're the same height, and his stride is longer. It takes him nineteen steps to reach first base from home plate. You take twenty-four usually."

"Show me."

Rinehart pulled his scissors from where he always kept them in a sheath with his dissecting knife—in case of emergency autopsies. He cut out a paper doll of me from his photographs. He cut out Monk. He laid them on the driveway grass. He touched all four legs with his scissors.

"No, I don't mean show me Monk's best. I mean show me how I can get better."

"You'll improve with practice. Start with your usual stride down the driveway." Rinehart fixed my sling tighter than ever against my body.

I ran the grassy strip from Military Road to our garage. I counted my steps. Twenty-four. Twenty-four every time for the ninety feet. Rinehart watched me from under the bill of his baseball cap. He said nothing about my stride, only about if my arm hurt. "Yes, even when I hold it still. Worse if I joggle it accidentally."

Rinehart measured the driveway again. With string, he marked lines for me to land on each step. "If today you add only one half inch to each stride, that adds up to twelve inches over the distance. A whole foot. How many times this season already have you been thrown out at first base by a foot?"

I thought back over our games. "Maybe five times."

Wizard Rinehart didn't lift his calculator from his briefcase. He said, "Being safe those times would bring your batting average up to .420. Now stretch your legs and hit these strings in the grass."

I stretched. I aimed at the marks. I hit some, not others, the first run. I hit more the second run. What helped me was concentrating. The third run I forced myself to think about my feet, not my arm. I hit more marks. It helped to see Rinehart standing there counting. He smiled more at me than at his stop-watch. My stride lengthened most when Rinehart warned me about placing my feet. "Point your toes so you run straight ahead. Don't let them flutter crooked. Straight. Straight," he said, not too loud because it was early Sunday morning. Every ninety feet Rinehart wrote in his log. How fast I ran. How many steps. My improvement in inches. He wrote what I complained about my arm, and after I finished running he sat me against the garage for a rest. He touched the lump on my shoulder. That hurt fiercely. Tears sprang to my eyes. I turned my head and cried.

Rinehart watched my eyes by squatting directly in front of me. He didn't look away. His voice sounded sadder than when his snake died. "What's this clear fluid sloshing down your cheeks?" He delved in his briefcase. He moved this and that. Finally he tore a page from his log. He crinkled it and wiped away clear fluid. "Up and at 'em, Zanboomer," he commanded in Coach O'Hara's same voice. "You'll feel better hitting the marks. And when you can lift your right arm you'll run faster and faster."

"When? When will I be good as new?" I already felt happier, crying on Rinehart's log.

Rinehart wouldn't promise. But he didn't hurry home to his mice, either. He stayed until his log got heavier from all that ink.

Chapter 12

SCIENTIFICA RINEHARTICULUM
Daily Log of Arthur Rinehart,
Volume IX, p. 112

Monday, May 8, 10:05 P.M.

After I talked to Dr. Ableson today, I found this statement in a medical book I "borrowed" from the Arlington County Hospital library:

IT IS MORE IMPORTANT TO KNOW WHAT KIND OF
PATIENT HAS AN INJURY THAN TO KNOW WHAT
KIND OF INJURY A PATIENT HAS.

These words give me hope. I know my patient better than Dr. Ableson and the orthopedic specialist do. They believe Zan will miss the rest of this season because of her shoulder. But science has no words for her determination to recover. She will! Sooner! No matter what they say.

I visited Dr. Ableson in his office at 3:30 P.M. At first he refused to answer my questions. He ushered me to the door. Those steps across his green rug reminded me of the grass yesterday, of Zan's spikes running until she exhausted herself. I stopped with my hand on his office doorknob. I announced, "Zan will die if she cannot play baseball."

Dr. Ableson did not say, "Let her die." He rolled his eyes at the ceiling. I suppose he resents autopsies. I repeated my original reason for the appointment with him: "I am Zan's best friend. I shall help her heal if I understand more about her injury." He asked me what I understood already. I read from this log certain passages I'd copied from *The American Journal of Sports Medicine.* I showed him drawings I'd done. He buzzed his nurse. She brought in a folder with HAGEN printed in blue. Those letters reminded me of Zan's name on her uniform. She must wear it soon, I thought while I copied information from her folder into my log.

The injury can be summarized in fewer words than Dr. Ableson's daily reports.

I Nomenclature of Zan's Athletic Injury: Acromio-clavicular sprain, 2nd degree.

II Additional Term: Acromioclavicular separation.

III Cause: Slide into home plate during high school game. Left foot across plate. Right arm back. Force of tag and contact with ground and with two bodies on right extended arm forced the humerus up against the glenoid and acromion, pushing them backward and the clavicle remaining forward so that stress was applied to the acromioclavicular and the coracoclavicular ligaments.

IV Symptoms: Acute local pain; disability.

V Signs: Prominence of joint; local tenderness; ligamentous and capsular laxity with increased mobility about joint.

VI X ray: Outer end of clavicle displaced slightly upward.

VII Pathology: Tear of acromioclavicular ligament but not of coracoclavicular ligaments.

VIII Treatment: Cold dressings; hot pressure dressings; arm in sling to bring downward pressure on clavicle. Sling to be worn 6 weeks, permitting ligaments to unite and become strong.

IX Rehabilitation: After removal of sling, program of range-of-motion exercises.

Dr. Ableson claims he "broke the news" to Zan this morning about how long she must wear her sling. She wouldn't believe him. He says she laughed when he told her she could "resume vigorous activity by August." Of course she knows that Lee High ends its baseball season the first week of summer.

Now I must decide how much I should reveal to Zan. To repeat Ableson's diagnosis will hinder her recovery. I must keep her spirits up, as well as my own. I must observe her psychological reactions to pain and stress for my science-fair project on athletic motivation.

Tuesday, May 9, 7:30 P.M.

Zan and I used the Lee track for running today. From there she could see her team, other side of the fence. For striding, she aimed at lines I'd marked along the straightaway. She pretended not to notice her former teammates, but often I was forced to wave my cap to bring back her attention from their boomers to her own legs. She tended to listen for Mr. O'Hara's orders to his team. To a large extent I have modeled my own coaching style on Mr. O'Hara's. Zan seems to respond well to his aloof sternness. Is this because she wants to play at any price? My observations of her sports motivation continue.

She says she cannot compete in tomorrow's game against Winchester County Day School. "The guys don't need me, anyway, to beat such a sissy school," she admitted to me. We have no transportation to the game. Zan feels that riding the team bus would be pushy of her out of uniform. "I'm useless to them," she ends all our discussions. I have resigned my position as unofficial Generals' photographer for the *Herald* to devote myself completely to Zan's comeback.

Wednesday, May 10, 2:30 P.M.

Zan no longer eats lunch at the Generals' training table. She feels it would be a "waste of good food." We sit together in another corner. This noon I drew a picture of her injury so she understands Dr. Ableson's big words. (See Appendix I, this log.) I reminded her that her ligament will heal faster than expected by those who don't really know her determination and my cure.

Thursday, May 11, 8:00 P.M.

The Generals defeated Winchester yesterday without her. Zan now foresees she will not be able to lift

103

her throwing arm for the doubleheader tomorrow against John Marshall High. She didn't cry when she told me. She complains that her arm hurts but claims that it "doesn't bother" her. (She is learning to live with pain.)

Mr. O'Hara invited Zan to play one honorary inning in the annual game this Saturday against Lee faculty—to remind fans that she has been a General. Zan asked him what help she could be. If I were O'Hara, I would have suggested Zan be sent in as a substitute runner. Her stride has lengthened. She hasn't mentioned this to anyone. We plan to keep her running improvement a secret until she's on the base paths again.

Sunday, May 14, 6:30 A.M.

Yesterday Mr. O'Hara allowed Zan to use the team's training room while they played Lee's faculty. I gave her legs a rubdown because she'd gone farther than our usual track workout. She had dashed around the neighborhood reminding students to vote Aileen Dickerson for prom queen. Aileen won last night. According to Mr. Mergler's Sunday headline: "RIGHT FIELDER SCORES ON DANCE FLOOR." Mergler notes, incidentally, that Aileen was thrown out stealing twice in the games Friday.

Sunday, May 14, 6:30 P.M.

When we came home to my laboratory from Zan's practice runs she wanted to borrow a book about

104

arms. I gave her *The Structure and Function of Human Bodies* from my growing collection. She read silently several hours. I moved every animal cage into the furnace room, providing lab space for my scientific observations of humans. I observed Zan feeling sad and guilty about not playing baseball. Why else would she cry while reading a scientific textbook?

Wednesday, May 17, 4:00 P.M.

In English, first period, Zan answered Fuzzy Harrison that she is writing her book report on "an arm and leg book, not on sports." Fuzzy nearly fainted. She gathered her wits (such as they are) and said a "medical book report would earn another A and certainly be as fascinating" as Zan's recent essay, "My Best Friend Helped Me Discover a Hobby Without Embarrassment All Summer."

In study hall, last period, Zan reminded me that my forged excuse for her had come true. "I do consult with my physician about various medical complications," she quoted my forgery. Then she asked for the three hundredth time, "When can I throw? Hit like I used to? How about this sling?" I answered by cinching the buckles tighter and noting her progress so far in running.

Monday, May 22, near midnight

Unable to make entries in log for five days. In addition to supervising Z's legs, have been writing and

105

printing *Rinehart's Science Newsletter*. The entire issue explores reasons for athletic participation. Money raised through sales will finance necessary equipment. Will also sell animals except those involved in diet experiments. Have already released insects and reptiles in Lubber Run Park.

Tuesday, May 23, 6:00 P.M.

It has been three weeks and twenty-three hours since my patient's injury occurred, and, although she has missed nine games, she seems as desperate as ever to rejoin the Generals. She begs me to raise and lower her arm, even if it kills her. I keep putting that off. Today she raised and lowered her feet instead, in the ankle weights I bought to strengthen her legs. I try to keep her mind on her legs.

Thursday, May 25, 6:00 P.M.

"Strength is power is speed." Zan chants this, lifting her ankle weights. It's a quote from *Human Physiology*.

Saturday, May 27, 9:45 A.M.

I am writing with one hand and timing Zan's sprints with the other. She insisted on a superhuman workout today. So far she's done every leg conditioner I've suggested:

1. weight training in lab
2. slow running to Lee track
3. running in small circles at 50-yard line
4. running figure eights around goalposts
5. runs up stadium steps in heavy hiking boots
6. sprints on track

This program will build up her ankles, knees, hips, and back. She used the end-zone grass for leg calisthenics. In another five minutes I will make her rest again and swallow salt tablets with eight ounces of water, thus replacing fluid she is losing.

10:30 A.M. same day

To continue. My patient just told me that while she's running hard she feels less useless. She knows her new speed will strengthen the Generals against Joe Donn. She knows the "burning" in her chest increases her lung capacity because she runs more laps every day "before the burning starts." She also said she feels lonely while she's running, not happy such as when she's playing a "real sport." She complained that no one cheers an alone runner or writes headlines and fan letters or shouts "Peanuts, popcorn," or sends pro scouts in folding chairs. Most of all she misses teammates. Specifically, she said, "In basketball games, kids run close beside you. In baseball you're either packed together in the dugout or moving near your teammates on the diamond. Sports huddles are the most fun. I can't wait to pile hands with my teammates like before."

All these statements help me understand Zan's motives for competing in sports. They also show she's hurting. So I piled my two hands on her good one. I blew my whistle festively and shouted, "Hot dawgs." For our next workout I shall bring a folding chair. Perhaps I can persuade Tammy Pam Tupper to write her first fan letter to a lonely runner. Or I shall forge one. Zan is composing her own book report, so I won't need to forge that.

Wednesday, May 31, 6:00 P.M.

Acting in my capacity as Zan's paraprofessional physician, I advised her *not* to remove her sling for the regular season's final inning tomorrow, the seventh inning of the unfinished Redskin game. My reasoning is this: The Generals have already earned a spot in next week's play-offs; therefore the conclusion of the game Zan was originally injured in will not matter in league standings. Each of the four remaining outs in that game will no doubt be savagely fought. Zan might be reinjured. In short, I urged her to save herself for play-off games ahead.

Thursday, June 1, 11:00 A.M.

For Zan's sake I am meeting her in the Generals' training room at noon. She begged me all the way to school to help her prepare for the Redskin inning today. She threatens to shuck off her sling "forever" if I'm not there.

Thursday, June 1, 2:30 P.M.

O'Hara found Zan waiting on the rubdown table before I arrived. He told her outright that one month is not long enough for positive healing of a ligament, hers or anyone's. He demanded that she stay buckled in her sling another two weeks. He apparently became gruff with Zan's pleas to play against Joe Donn this afternoon. She wouldn't tell what else he said but I heard "A coach's task is to win games with healthy athletes, not to coddle injured ones!" He shouted that as she left.

Study hall is quieter than usual. Most students went to a parking-lot pep rally for the Generals before they board their bus for Richmond. Zan sits in front of me, writing her book report. She says her eyes are too red for pepping the team. She claims her sling "looks grungy." She doesn't want to mix with crowds. Kids look at her "funny." Zan says they don't remember she was ever a General.

Sunday, June 4, near midnight

All weekend Zan mourned. She feels guilty about the Generals' loss to Richmond. She feels they may lose again in the series if she hasn't regained her "premier condition." She stopped talking after those confessions to me. She never carries her glove anymore. But she hasn't stopped running. She followed my instructions about improving her body angle. She now keeps her head up, her ankles, hips, shoulders, and head in a straight line. Of course, she cannot pump her right arm in a push/pull rhythm until it is out of the sling. I have given my word we will try certain arm motions tomorrow, here in my lab following weight training. I must sell every piece of equipment not directly related to Zan's comeback in order to make space for rehabilitation weights.

Nearer midnight

Zan just phoned. She can't sleep, as usual. Worrying about her shoulder and the play-offs causes insomnia, or at least that is my diagnosis. As her personal physician I explained she needed to tire herself out. I advised her to run around the block for twenty minutes or so. Running is my usual prescription for her! Healthy legs help her forget she can't boom.

Midnight

Zan phoned again. While she ran she thought of another reason she loves sports. She not only misses teammates, she misses enemies. She's sick of running because there's no one to run *with* or *against*. This observation fits with my theories ("Revenge Among Athletes") in next week's *Newsletter*. Further money will purchase a complete set of weights and running shoes for Zan. Her spikes have nearly worn through to her foot from running on pavement. She's saving them now for the play-offs and series.

I am trying to remain unemotional about Zan's injury. Even though my hand is shaking I shall continue recording scientifically the physical and psychological progress of my patient.

One hour ago I removed Zan's sling. Watching her face, I saw no sign of pain. I lowered her arm slowly to her side. I asked her to make the following arm movements: slight backward extensions; slight forward flexions. These gave only a "little" pain. I returned her arm to the neutral position, straight down at her side. She started lifting it before I called "Lift slowly." Gritting her teeth, she brought her arm halfway horizontal to her shoulder. She said this didn't hurt, but I detected a certain amount of pain in her eyes. She complained of stiffness, not soreness, during gentle rotations of her arm. So far, so good.

But—she could not swing her new bat. She failed to throw a BB across my laboratory. From being in a sling so long, her arm and shoulder muscles are tight. She has not recovered her complete range of motion. "When?" Zan asked her favorite question. She thought that once the sling disappeared she would be her usual boomer self. I had not led her to believe otherwise. I stalled for an answer to "When?" To divert her, I drew another picture of her shoulder, now it has healed. (See Appendix II, this log.) I listed exercises and weight routines to improve her weakened muscles. I recommended that she continue wearing her sling another week except during workouts. I couldn't look her in the eyes right then. I gazed at the calendar and reminded Zan that she's one week ahead of Dr. Ableson's schedule. I promised—yes, promised—to have her ready for the Virginia State Series if her Generals survive play-offs.

"Dream on," Zan said and ran away.

Saturday, June 10, early evening

I lent Zan my wristwatch to time her nightly runs around the block. She asked for it. Five days of rehabilitative exercises (mainly shoulder shrugs, upright rowing, and dumbbell presses) have lifted her spirits and loosened her muscles. She can throw a tennis ball across Glebe Road. Her bat follows through the lab strike zone I constructed of string.

While she worked out, Zan listened to play-offs on my radio. (I was busy counting her repetitions.) The Generals have eked their way into Round 3. They barely defeated Roanoke and Appomattox in away games.

Sunday, June 12, during morning workout

Mergler's column featured news of every Redskin play-off win. Zan cut out the *Herald* picture of Joe Donn Joiner and played paper dolls with her enemy. She threw golf balls at him. She oiled him in the pocket of her glove. She carried him along to Lee track and sprinted past him every quarter mile. I never saw any athlete so psyched up. Zan'll definitely be in that series!

Monday, June 12, late

Today, six weeks after her injury, Zan visited Dr. Ableson to have her sling officially removed. I cinched it tighter than ever, before we left study hall. I waited in the hospital library. Zan says Ableson put her through the same motion tests I used a week ago. She says he couldn't believe that her trapezius, pectoral, deltoid, and latissimus muscles were so loose and supple. He pronounced her halfway able to play fall sports. I heard her laughing three doors away.

Thursday, June 15, who knows when

For the sake of science I shall write one last log entry, even though my heart is breaking.

In our secret workout this morning at Lee Stadium, Zan threw a baseball from shallow shortstop to second base. I ducked. Then I bowled her the ball. She managed to bunt me grounders. She pushed hits back at me and ran them out. Much encouraged, we jogged home to our lab for daily weight lifting. Zan talked excitedly about how surprised Joe Donn Joiner would be when she clicked up the dugout steps to boom him on Saturday in the series opener.

So far, so good.

But—in their concluding play-off game this afternoon against Bristol Consolidated High School, the Generals lost dismally. Thus they are out of the Virginia State Series. Bristol, not Zan, will play the Redskins.

After all our work! After Zan's struggle for a comeback. After my schemes to keep us both from retirement. I have no more schemes. I must think. I can't face Zan. I give up.

APPENDIX I

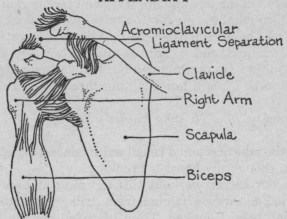

Acromioclavicular Ligament Separation

Clavicle

Right Arm

Scapula

Biceps

APPENDIX II

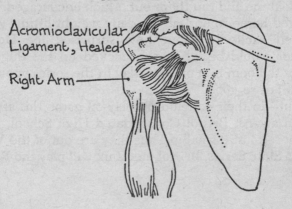

Acromioclavicular Ligament, Healed

Right Arm

Chapter 13

Summer began without me. I hid in bed all day. I told Mom my legs fizzled from six weeks of running for nothing.

The only human organ that really hurt was my broken heart a lot. What if I'd played against Bristol? I might could've scored that three-run difference. I should've ignored the pain more and lifted my arm sooner. I let the Generals down. I shouldn't've listened to Rinehart about legs. He distracted me.

I blinked away guilty tears. Poor Monk had wanted that winners' ring bad. Aileen had counted on prom queen *and* state series. I'd failed them.

Mom served me dinner on a tray. I didn't feel hungry, but I ate and faced up to what I had to do— totally forget about baseball or else end up asking "What if?" all summer. What if I'd yanked off my sling sooner? Maybe my old teammates would be winners now instead of Richmond. What if Rinehart had schemed better how to cure me? Then in the series last weekend I'd've destroyed Joe Donn with my new Slugger and stride. What if?

Anyway, I had my faster legs. I'd save them for baseball next year. Nine months to the new season! Wait all that time to boom. To win. Misery.

I jumped out from under the bedspread, grabbed my glove from where it hung over my desk, and buried it way to the bottom of my sweat-shirt drawer. I rolled my bat through dustballs in the closet. I heaved my spikes into the laundry hamper. They could rust there for all I cared. I'd go barefoot if I ever left my room again. Then Mom would stop complaining how I ruined her rugs by wearing spikes around our house and practicing slides under the piano.

I lay down to wipe tears on the bedspread. I sniffled about Rinehart's cure. Anyway, he meant well. He'd ditched his animals for me. He'd kept my hopes up. He'd meant better than all those kids who sent me get-well cards and forgot me. Injuries make has-beens out of athletes. That's it. I'm a has-been.

I leafed through the Lee High yearbook to find my old self. For pages kids' stony faces stared into my sad one. Fuzzy's hair filled most of her space in the English department, but I sort of liked her tonight. She'd given me A on my unforged book report. Ditto Dr. Semler in science. He couldn't believe all I knew about the parts of my body for his semester exam. "Miss Hagen's injury and rehabilitation taught her something besides spheres," he announced to the class.

Sure. Sure. I learned I didn't have permanent teammates.

I turned to the yearbook's sport section. I paused at our baseball picture. I barely recognized myself. I grinned in March. I looked fatter, more special in a uniform. All us players looked important. And happier than after the final loss to Bristol. Every General bawled that game. We bawled again our last day of school when all the kids signed yearbooks and said "See ya" for the summer. E.J. had already left for camp up in Vermont. My other infield pals were gone, too. Monk went backpacking in the Blue Ridge; Eugene hitched to Bethany Beach for work with a construction company. Aileen would spend another week ironing her wardrobe, but then move to Ocean City until September. Randy, our only senior, couldn't wait for graduation night. He'd signed a contract for pro ball and reported to Norfolk.

That leaves me four ex-teammates in Arlington, enough for playing pepper games. . . .

I knew I'd never see them until the day after Labor Day. Ben had a job as swimming-pool manager at Potomac Golf and Country Club. Jumbo's lifeguard there. They both stay until dark, when Fritz arrives as night watchman. He drives around the golf course in a pink Jeep, chasing vandals and turning sprinklers on and off. DumDum would be working for Ben except our right fielder failed two classes. He has to make them up at summer school to keep eligible for football.

I ate my dessert. I thought about summer and ate my heart out.

That leaves me my best friend. Rinehart's vacation in Maine isn't until August. But he can't hit baseballs to me or catch. He's a sports bust. And a loner. He isn't on any team in the whole yearbook or in any club, not even the biology club.

I found Rinehart's picture way at the end, standing in front of his last year's winning project: cages full of butterflies. He'd taught those bugs to chase a mov-

117

ing target. He'd taught them all different flight patterns. He'd made them into speed fiends instead of slow flutterers. His picture smiled at me. His thick glasses glinted. "Nothing's hopeless to a man of science," I could hear him saying. He sure can buck a guy up. He could probably teach *me* to fly this summer, say he had time.

I slid the dinner tray onto my bureau. I dropped the yearbook behind my bookcase so I'd lay off thinking team. I paced my strange room. I couldn't recognize it. My baseball treasures were hidden forever for nine months. OOOps. My cap. Slam it in the closet. Let moths chew LEE off. Flick out lights. Go to sleep. Forget.

Misery. July and August without team sports. Plus September, October, and November with only badminton and volleyball. No state finals in sight. No revenge. No booms.

Misery. I can't sleep. It should be easy. For a change, my baseball glove isn't a lump under my pillow. I'm getting used to no sling buckles poking me. But when I shut my eyes, curves and sliders dip over the plate. I'd better get up and run to wear myself out. Before that I'd better write Rinehart a letter to thank him for telling me how to fall asleep with a mind full of gloom. I haven't seen him in days. Maybe he's mad at me for not helping the Generals. He hasn't phoned. He probably blames me that I didn't recover faster. He hasn't come over. He hasn't mailed me a scheme, even. I better write him first. "Dear Rinehart," I put on notebook paper. I scratched that out. "Dear Arthur" seemed nicer.

"Dear Personal Paraphysician" seemed stuffy. "Dear Pal. Dear Only Friend Who Helped Me." My pen slipped on clear fluid.

Rinehart deserves my best handwriting. I'd write when I came home from my run. Or probably I wouldn't. It's summer, microscope time in his cozy lab. Rinehart's eyes are too busy for me.

I pulled on my sweat suit over my pajamas. I wore old basketball shoes, Keds with thick rubber soles. I snuck out the kitchen door, through the garage, ran up the grassy strip to Military Road. Along Military to Thirtieth Street. Up Thirtieth Street hill. Thanks to Rinehart I ran easily, with longer strides and plenty of breath. "Dear Rinehart," I wrote in my head. "You trained me for this. My legs give me hope. Thank you. Sincerely, Zanboomer." My mind crossed out "boomer," running along the country-club fence. I crossed out "Dear Rinehart" and thought "Dear Coach" because I remembered his clipboard and cap. In our driveway again I checked the wristwatch he'd lent me and saw I ran ten seconds ahead of my time last night. Six minutes flat from our garage door, around the block, and touch the door. I'll ask Rinehart to figure how far with his tape measure. Six minutes for how many feet or miles per street? I might run the block faster in daytime when I could see farther ahead and not worry about stepping into potholes. Also, I'd run faster if the whole block went downhill. Sure, faster. Running faster is fun.

I took off my shoes so I wouldn't wake up the house. Carrying them, I noticed how heavy they felt.

119

Heavy shoes—slow feet. Lighter me—faster me. I learned that from Eugene's diet. His third basing improved with pounds he lost, especially his running game. From hauling bricks this summer he would shed weight. He'd build muscles. Strength is power is speed. By football season Eugene would be a super fullback.

When school started up after Labor Day what would I be? A has-been shortstop! Misery. No one to play baseball with now. No fall sport that lets me boom.

In my room I checked myself out under my sweat suit. For sure I'm thinner from running every day. From loss of appetite and no Pepsis away from my teammates. But my thighs feel more muscly when I sock them. My calves, my bicepses femoris seem to show more. "Dear Rinehart," I started another letter at my desk. "You built my legs up. Now teach me to fly this summer."

Fly for what?

Misery. Under the lamp on my bed table I kept my enemy collection, paper dolls from the *Herald*. At least I had these. An enemy's better than no teammate. I examined each guy, hoping he'd spook me to sleep: Joe Donn Joiner, all slimy from my glove oil; Dwayne Yelverton, out of his squat for a change, crossing first base in the series. What a stride he has. I'll ask Rinehart to measure it. I'll ask him if I could beat Dwayne and Joe Donn in a foot race next game we play. Next April in a grudge match! All those months before I get even. Misery. "Dear Rinehart. You collected my tears to analyze under your microscope. What did they tell you? P:S. Here's some more."

Midnight on Rinehart's wristwatch. The red numbers flashed 12:01, 12:02. I kept time in the dark. I thought about time. Seasons. Summer. Months. Misery. Weeks. Days. Minutes. Seconds.

"Dear Coach. I have discovered a new enemy— every runner's enemy. Time."

Chapter 14

Tammy P. Tupper
2184 Wilson Boulevard
Arlington, Virginia
June 21

Suzanne Hagen
587 Military Road
Arlington, Virginia

Dearest Zanboomer!

I do not write fan letters in summer usually.

There are no Generals then.

But you are a General all by yourself. You are a team of one.

I see you running along Military Road.

I love how fast you go, faster every night.

Your legs boom on the pavement.

Please send me your magic shoes. I shall place them with Aileen Dickerson's curl in my own sports hall of fame.

Good luck in your race.

XXXXXXOOOOOOO
Tammy Pam

Chapter 15

Rinehart's forgery got me out of bed early and downstairs to the phone.

"I deny this charge," he said in his sincerest voice. "I do not write Tammy Pam's fan letters."

"Rinehart, I'm positive it's from your laboratory. Admit so I can fall back in bed. My ventricles ache."

A silence came over the phone, strange for Rinehart. After a while he said, "Zanner, I meant well. How could you tell I forged it?"

"Tons of clues. Tammy would never see me running late at night. She's only nine years old. And she's away on vacation with the other Tupper sisters."

Rinehart whispered, "Curses," like some nutty scientist when a test tube boils over.

"You signed hugs and kisses in capital letters. Tammy sent small ones to every teammate. Me she sent none."

"I'm more generous than a Tupper. I'm delighted you noticed."

"Plus Aileen didn't mail Tammy a curl. She kept them thick for the prom."

"You really should mail Tammy your heavy Keds for her whatnot shelf. I'll buy you lightweight running shoes from my *Newsletter* fund. We could choose them this morning."

"I'm sleeping. After that I'm rearranging my own

baseball keepsakes into oblivion. After that, running to sleep."

I'll say this for Rinehart: He *never* gives up. He stuck on the phone persuading me to meet him halfway, at Clarendon Sports Shop. He said if I wore running shoes I wouldn't get heel spurs, black toenails, fallen arches, fungus infections, blisters, tibial varus. The twenty-six bones in my feet would thank me, he said. I'd look like a champion. I'd win races.

"A champion what? Which races? I need new house slippers for my season in bed."

"Meet me and I'll give you sports enemies to add to your collection."

More enemies sounded better than being lonesome. And if I met Rinehart at the store I could tell him about his electric wristwatch as an enemy. I could ask him to scheme me up a whole sports summer.

Okay, we met. I hurried through the baseball section, not peeking. In another room an entire wall of shoes on display confused me but not Rinehart. He'd brought a catalogue in his briefcase. He wouldn't let me near soccer shoes or shot-put shoes even though I wanted two of everything. Because I loved the colors! Because I loved the stripes! Each pair had different numbers of stripes going in different directions. Because I loved the two-tone mixtures of nylon and suede or suede and smooth leather! "I'll take them! I'm versatile. I'll play every sport alone this summer."

"Please bring her these Tigers and these Pumas," Rinehart asked the man who waited for me to decide. I might've known my pal would fall for animal brands. I couldn't complain. Both pairs fit snugly. Rinehart said what I thought. "Pumas seem sturdy, durable. Nylon will dry fast if you run in wet grass. Soles will absorb road shock. Tigers seem flexible. The color is more or less Generals blue."

"I like those orange ones up there."

"They're Nikes," the man told me, yanking a pair my size from the wall.

"We'll take them."

Rinehart hadn't pressed the Nikes to figure out where my toes came. He hadn't inspected heel lifts, upper softness, interior support, outer soles, or the other notes he'd written in his log. Without blinking he counted $33.95 plus tax from his briefcase and forked it over to the cash register—more money than my bat and baseball cost together. Outside the store, I asked him why.

"You like orange Nikes, that's enough. You're the one who's going to run hundreds of miles in them. And no other team in your league wears orange. You're a team of one, as Tammy said."

With the tissue paper and box and gift wrap, my shoes still felt lighter than meringue. I swung the bag, walking home. I felt happier.

"Moreover," Rinehart said, "Nike was the Greek goddess of victory. How's that for a head start?"

Head start on who? Hundreds of miles? Team of one? "I'll pay back your money," I said quickly, not wanting to guess what Rinehart had schemed up for me those six days I hadn't seen him. Probably some weird sport his emaciated white mice play. I changed the subject to wristwatches. I explained how every night my trip around the block went faster.

"No doubt, since you can use both arms to help pull the hill."

"What if there weren't a hill? I could run faster, right?"

Rinehart stopped in his tracks. "There will be hills. Higher than Thirtieth Street. There will be surfaces skiddier than asphalt. Rocky Redskin Stadium clogged with soda cans and bullies was a goose-down pillow compared to a cross-country racecourse." He balanced his briefcase across one raised knee. He handed me two new guys, not flimsy like my cutouts from the *Herald*. His were newspaper photos, all right, but he'd mounted them on cardboard. He'd used his autopsy kit to trim around their faces, so they weren't jagged like Joe Donn's, cut with Mom's pinking shears. I checked out their eyes. They didn't seem hard like Dwayne's. They seemed to be hurting. They seemed to be pleading "Stop." Their feet had Tigers and Pumas like on the store wall. They also wore shorts and mix-matching shirts with no names, just numbers. Their arms churned. Their legs stretched in wide strides.

"They're running," I said.

"They're runners."

"What sport?"

"Cross-country racing."

"Never heard of it. Where's their team? I'll put them all in my collection."

"No teams. Only one guy per school enters this race. It's the Virginia Cross-Country Championship

126

in November. Lee High didn't send a runner last year. Or the year before. Ever. I looked up old records in the *Herald* morgue."

I dumped Rinehart's paper-doll runners in with the shoes. I twirled them around together. "What're these guys' names?" I asked when we were nearly at my house.

"Names aren't important. It's numbers that count. Times. Times they take to cover miles." Rinehart ambled down Wilson Boulevard. At the curb he set his briefcase on a crosswalk line. "Cross-country racing seems like a simpleminded sport. It takes place in city parks or on fields out in the country. Thirty runners or fifty or seventy-five—any old imprecise number—stand behind a white line like this. They wait for a gun to be fired. At the shot, all these human bodies charge forward to race along a marked trail. Through woods. Up hills. Over streams. Racecourses always differ. Looks like fun. Like a kids' game—a picnic. No dangerous curveballs to boom. No hockey sticks to avoid. Easy. The only purpose is for one runner to go fastest for three miles or four or five, whatever the length of the course."

I opened my shoe bag, glanced at the paper dolls. Their mouths hung crooked.

Rinehart read from his log: "Distance cannot be charmed or cheated. There is no way around it. A timed race of known length provides an unarguable measure of skill, physical condition, and willpower."

Rinehart used his softest voice for reading aloud. I thought about distance and time, same as I did last night. I decided to impress my pal. "I ran my block in six minutes last night."

"Six minutes and how many seconds? I lent you my watch for precision."

"No seconds."

"A six-minute mile? Not bad. Considering the hill, your basketball shoes, the dim streetlamps, your lack of training. Could you do it again?"

I answered by unwrapping my shoes. I owed Rinehart once around the block for rousing me out of bed today, the second day of my sportsless summer. I owed him for these nameless enemies—for his new scheme. It must be vicious. It's taken him a week alone to figure. I owe him for these orange shoes with pinpoint ventilating holes to keep my feet cool hundreds of miles of his scheme. I noticed the word "Nike" written big on the heel. That ought to scare those two guys in a cross-country race if I ever run one. Maybe that's why their eyes hurt. They've seen Nikes ahead of them. I placed the paper dolls beside me on my starting line.

Rinehart bent down. "Run facing traffic to Thirtieth. Run tall uphill, not slumping forward. Turn into Pollard. Stay close to the golf-course fence. Down Thirty-first Street. Lean forward and lengthen your stride downhill. Let fly back to this line." Rinehart raked his heel through gravel.

I'd show Rinehart some speed. He wasn't fooling me with his forged fan letter, his $33.95 plus tax, and this race against myself. He'd drawn my first starting line. My legs are about to go into cahoots with his head.

128

"Go," Rinehart called. His stopwatch clicked.

I went because I wanted to show myself some speed, more than last night. Much more than a week ago, my sleepless night after the Bristol game when I couldn't see too good with my dumb leaking eyes. I'll prove to myself I've got skill, conditioning, and willpower, I thought, striding past the next-door neighbor's lawn, lawn after lawn. My familiar course wasn't so different in daylight. And I started getting winded at the same fire hydrant as ever.

Thirtieth Street hill loomed suddenly on my left. Turn sharp left. Don't waste steps in a wide swing. Conquer the hill without slowing. Last night I eased up around here. Not today. Run faster. How to run faster? Don't slow down. Don't say to myself here's a hard part, go easy and save breath for other streets. How to run faster? Tell legs faster, faster. Think about nothing but speed. Concentrate. Like baseball. No, don't think about baseball. Think up. Up.

I thought up. Faster.

Halfway uphill I felt the usual stitch in my side. Two-thirds up I decided to stop at the top, grab a light pole, and wait for the bus. Up. I didn't let up. At the crest I didn't hesitate. I got right back in my flat-ground stride and turned into Pollard Street. Sure, so I didn't have breath. So I had a stitch. Only two more streets home. Run!

The country-club fence stretched forever on my right. On my left, the end house looked like a dot, far away in Texas. Pretend it's close. Psych up. I'm leading this race. I've led from the word "go." Joe Donn and Dwayne didn't enter. Those other two paper dolls never broke off the line. They're face down in blacktop, their hurt eyes dodging my win.

I know why their eyes hurt. Running hurts. I hurt. All over me, worse than my arm used to.

Texas's coming closer. I'll pause there for a drink from the birdbath. I'm slowing. Running fast causes every inch of the body to suffer. Run faster, suffer more, beat the stopwatch. Stride out. Rinehart's at my house with an oceanful of Pepsi, never mind bird water. Hurt one more block, then take a carbonated bath.

My thumbs don't hurt. Think about thumbs while turning down Thirty-first Street. Bomb downhill. Don't rest, even though you deserve it after running this far this fast. Tilt forward from the waist. Go up on toes. Down. Down with heavy legs, heavier than this station wagon driving toward me. Hope it sees me. My eyes are sweaty. Oh-oh, my thumbs ache now. My body's shot. I can't keep running.

Except to the finish line. My hair doesn't hurt. Think about hair.

Hair.

Faster.

Shoelaces coming untied. Lungs busting through ribs. Bear down, fellow.

Oh, no. What's that string ahead. Across Military Road. Tied to our mailbox. Duck it—duck—

"Break it, Zanboomer."

The string clung to my forehead as I slowed up and stopped. Rinehart had released his end because the string didn't break. He said, "It breaks in books I've been reading all week." I clutched onto a tree in our front yard. My heart banged against the bark. I sucked in air like a dying donkey. That's me. I'm an ass to run a mile flat out.

Rinehart dangled his stopwatch under my eye, the eye without salt caked over in a stinging crust. "Five minutes, forty seconds, and six tenths."

I saw 5:40.6.

Right then I wanted to lop off the .6. After all, I'd left the starting line slowly, in bad shape from bed-ridden days sulking. I loafed on Military Road, enjoying the lawns. I'd slid sideways on grass cuttings. I'd had to drag my heels out of melting tar. I'd seen that dime in the gutter and almost bent to pick it up.

Only 5:40.6! I could run faster. Give me air and a drink and I'll think of other alibis. I'm not used to the Nikes. It's humid today. No teammates cheered me.

Rinehart sprayed the hose on me and my tree. My body cooled but my mind didn't. I schemed a faster race. I could do that mile in under 5:30, no sweat. Probably it was more than a mile. It felt longer. "Coach, how come you're sure I ran a mile?"

"I measured your course with a bicycle-wheel gauge I invented. Each street is a quarter mile." Rinehart gave me salt tablets and a nozzle of water. He gave me a compliment he'd stolen from the Generals: "Waytogo. Way to tough it out, Boomer." Sounded funny from a scientist.

Compliments work on me, though. I swore to myself I'd practice that hill in ankle weights from Rinehart's lab. I'd run every day in July to lower my time to 5:29.0. "My pancake breakfast weighed heavy as fish sinkers in my stomach," I mentioned. "If I'd

131

known I was racing today I wouldn't've eaten."

"Tomorrow you'll run before breakfast."

"Just promise I won't hurt as much as today."

"You'll hurt more."

"How can a guy hurt more?"

"From running faster. Do you want to know how fast your new enemies run a mile?"

I did.

I didn't.

I did.

"If you tell me, I'll run with their time in mind—I'll train harder August."

"You'll push yourself! I'll push you! Your workouts won't ever again be once around the block."

"Sounds better than pulling tufts out of my chenille bedspread all summer."

Rinehart didn't laugh at me. He said, "By September you'll run with guys' elbows in your rib cage."

"Whose?"

"We'll enlist competitors for practice, flesh-and-blood runners, not paper dolls. They'll have longer legs than yours. Stronger muscles. Smoother form. They'll be mean. Technically—"

"I'll lose."

"You'll win."

"On what? On my feet in your Greek goddess shoes? I'm not Aileen, the Queen."

"On this." Rinehart tapped my forehead. "You win races there. You think yourself across the finish line. Concentration, willpower—you have amounts greater than anyone."

"How do you know?"

132

"I watched you come back from your shoulder separation, remember?"

"I didn't come back."

"You're back now!" Rinehart adjusted his slipping-off glasses and looked me over from sopping hair to Nikes. "You're back even after I gave up last week. There—I've said it."

I let go the tree and sat down. Rinehart's confession hurt me more than my stitch. He didn't seem embarrassed. He didn't squint like into his microscope. He told me straight out that when the Generals lost to Bristol he'd locked his lab and thrown the key away for good into his briefcase. He'd felt useless. He'd "yielded to despair."

"Me too."

"No you didn't, Zan. You ran your course every night, as before," Rinehart said positively.

"Only to quit hitting dreamboomers. I ran to defeat insomnia."

"Wrong. You ran faster every night. You attempted to better your own times. You competed." Rinehart knelt in the wet grass. In his log he found a column of numbers. "Your times: 6:15.7

6:13.9

6:11.0."

So what? I thought about Rinehart's best blue suit getting green knees. He'd dressed special just to help me at the shoestore. To look official like a coach. For sure he hadn't given up. He'd measured my course. He'd concealed himself around here and timed me to a tenth second. "Rinehart, you never gave up. Swear."

"Yes, until I saw you stumbling this road after the Bristol win. And the next night not stumbling but sprinting. Your instinct is always to improve, to try harder whatever sport you're doing." Rinehart leafed through his log. "My white mice—each of my ex-animals—ran or wiggled or flew for food. Faster for food they liked best. But you're more complex than the creatures who used to live in my basement. I theorized you played ball for crowds; for team-mates' approval and for O'Hara's; for vengeance against teams that threatened the Generals. All that glory comprised your food, so to speak. You believe those reasons, don't you?"

I only half listened to my pal. I watched his Generals-blue tie turning limp in June humidity. He must be overheating to death in his wooly suit. I told him, "Crawl underneath this tree. Spread some shade on your mastermind." Rinehart dragged the hose with him. He cleaned his glasses. I washed salt from my eyes. We both took care not to drench his log. I turned pages past charts of race times, reviewing Rinehart's secrets. "What other theories did you dope out about me?" I asked when I found blanks.

"I've arrived at no conclusions as yet. I'm honestly perplexed." He shook his head. "If you don't run faster for fans, for friends, for enemies, then why?" he asked. "If you run only to improve—to improve for what?"

"Rinehart, your brain works overtime."

"What goes on in yours?"

"Well—I hit mental homers. I catch fictitious grounders." Rinehart seemed disappointed that I couldn't explain myself, so I added his new scheme. "Oh, I beat racers to imaginary finish lines."

"The Virginia Cross-Country Championship line is real enough. I'll coach you over it scientifically. I'll study your motivation. No more newts for me. I'll unravel a human mystery: What makes Zan boom?"

"Maybe I'll beat you to the answer."

Chapter 16

Then summer started over again for me and lasted six hundred miles. I counted them on the run. I'd write them down in Rinehart's log soon after I limped home from workouts. Those daily miles added up. Rinehart says my summer holiday's total is the same distance as from Arlington County to Maine. Or from one side of Texas to the other. He told me one morning, when I refused to put on my shoes, that famous cross-country runners—the ones in his books—run five thousand miles a year in practice. That's nearly coast to coast to coast, U.S.A.

He figured my miles out some sportier ways than on maps. Take the Robert E. Lee track, for instance. Four times around it makes a mile. Two thousand, four hundred times around makes six hundred miles. Or take my old baseball diamond. Home plate around to home plate is 120 yards. There are 1,760 yards in a mile. I'd need to hit 8,800 homers to run six hundred miles on the base paths. In football I'd need to score 10,560 touchdowns, end zone to end zone.

Rinehart figured. We both counted. But I did the running. From June 23 until Labor Day—six hundred miles.

June I ran before breakfast, before cars came out and the sun got too hot. I'd wake up hearing soft slaps. Slap. Slap. Drowsily I'd think of Pumas in front of me, going away. Slap. Slap. I'd think of Tigers behind me, gaining ground. More slaps. Fully awake, I'd remember Rinehart down in the yard. He'd be slapping his tree-branch alarm clock against my bedroom window. No end to his slaps unless I'd open the front door, dressed for running except my Nikes. Rinehart always tied them. He knew a sailor's knot that couldn't come loose, no matter what. "Shoes and surfaces, a runner's only equipment," he'd say and assign me my morning surface. Once around the block, slow and easy. Then rest by walking for a minute. Twice around the block, fast. Rest. Dash 100 yards straight along Military Road. Turn. Dash back. Repeat until winded. Rest. Repeat until heavy-legged. Rest. Repeat until totaled. Rest.

Rest, and listen to Rinehart's plans for the championship. Besides my training, based on how college racers train, we'd have to study my opponents, their styles of racing. We'd look them up in old newspapers and read the descriptions. We'd have to study the racecourse, which wouldn't be announced until October, during cross-country season. We'd have to forge my entry blank. He'd explain later.

"I hope it's a smarter forgery than your Tammy fan letter."

"That worked. I knew you'd catch me—my scheme within a scheme. After I gave up, my phony forgery brought us together."

"You call this together? I'm running. You're sitting."

"I'm thinking."

Rinehart thought up a different course for me every June morning. He predicted I'd get bored running the same old miles. He changed my scenery. His seat stayed the same: a lawn chair in our front yard, where he read books about racing.

I ran Military Road to Lee Highway and back, three miles of gentle hills. I ran Military Road in the other direction, to Chain Bridge and back. Tough hills and sharp curves. I ran Marcy Road in deep sand shoulders. I ran Glebe Road on silky cement sidewalks. I loped back and forth from my house to Rinehart's, from my house to school. I charged Thirtieth Street hill, up twelve times, with a jogging rest to warm down.

Warm down and answer Rinehart's scientific questions for his study of a solo athlete's motivation. "Tell me the hardest part of training," he said after a week of it.

"Putting my shoes on, knowing what's coming."

"What's coming?"

"Pain. My legs start out stiff every morning. Just when they limber up, my arms get tired from swinging. Just when I forget about them, my chest throbs and a stitch happens in my side. The sweat mustache around my mouth cracks. Heat gives me a headache. Speed gives me a stomachache. You've noticed me bending over for breath? You've watched me holding on to anything taller? What's coming is pain."

Rinehart jots "muscle fatigue," "heat stress and exhaustion," and "underdeveloped cardiovascular system." His log lies in wait for my next answer. "Why do you run?" he asks daily at almost the same time, depending on how far I've gone and how fast.

I never have the correct answer. Mostly I've learned what not to say. Not Lurleen. Not Generals. Not O'Hara. Not the *Herald*.

"I run to get it over with," I said on July 1, after a cruel six miles to Clarendon and back.

"You're not finished today. This evening you graduate to twice-a-day workouts. Long, slow distance each morning. Intervals at Lee track as the air cools off before dinner. See you at five."

No you won't. I'm tired. No way I'll be there. Nohow. Nowhere, as Joe Donn would say. Where is that creep right now, with his series rings on each hand? For sure he's not running like an aching moron in Richmond. Could I beat him my course around the block? Who cares! Do I care? I'll ask Rinehart later when I run against his stopwatch.

At five o'clock I ran Rinehart's intervals at the deserted Lee High track. Not even a caretaker hung on the fence to discover me using school property. I jogged a mile, four times around, to ease my stiffness. I did stretching exercises on the infield dirt. I stripped down to my nylon shorts and tank top. I wasn't about to haul extra cloth those intervals, not an ounce. I rested before the pain.

Rested and sipped plain water from a canteen Rinehart supplied. I inspected other goodies in his running kit: shoelaces, tape, Vaseline, Mungdrops, salt tablets, elastic knee wraps, a sweater. No books. He wasn't reading this afternoon, anything except his stopwatch. Click.

I dashed 220 yards. Walked 220. Dashed 220,

walked 220. Sounds simple until Rinehart calls "Faster" and reads off the times: 34.5 seconds; 33.9 seconds. "Faster." Dash 220 yards, walk 220 yards. Say to myself, "Faster, faster." Then 32.5 seconds; 32.3 seconds; 29.7 seconds. Rest.

Rest and ask my own questions. "Could Joe Donn run 220 yards in twenty-nine seconds?"

"Easily. He'd do one hundred yards in twelve seconds with all his football equipment on. With track shoes, he'd do two hundred and twenty in at least twenty-five seconds. He's noted as a breakaway quarterback."

"Will I ever get trained enough to beat him?"

"Perhaps not at sprints. But long-distance races—a mile, two miles cross-country—they're different. Training harder than rivals pays off. Being thin and small-boned helps. And of course this."

Rinehart tapped my forehead.

I asked, "Rinehart, in my mind do I want to beat Joe Donn?"

"That question's interesting but useless. Joe Donn won't be competing cross-country this fall. He plays football. Put your brain to work on today's problem: psyching up for intervals. These short sprints will build your wind. Talk to yourself as you run. Say, 'Faster, stronger, harder.' If you concentrate on speed, your body won't feel pain as soon. Mental fatigue sets in before physical fatigue."

"Faster! Stronger! Harder!"—29.6; 28.8; 28.6.

I ran and Rinehart coached. He abandoned his easy chair in mornings and followed my rambles on his bike. "We're dragging Main," he'd say when we hit Wilson Boulevard and turned toward Roslyn. "We're surveying Arlington County, street by street." He pedaled spastically with his eyes on the speedometer or on his stopwatch. The bike wobbled. He caught his pants in the chain. "Keep running, I'll repair it," he usually said. The rest of the time he said, "Keep running faster."

Long, slow distance became six miles, seven miles, and ten miles one morning when Rinehart decided to give me a preview of August. I ran the first mile with knees a little sore from the day before. The second mile I gushed sweat, but Rinehart pedaled one-handed and dried my face and neck. Miles three, four, and five I sailed, pain-free, with breath to chat. I didn't watch my feet or the buildings passing. I didn't count footfalls or telephone poles. I didn't think about speed until Rinehart said, "Pick up the pace." He handed me a plastic bottle of water. On and off for a half mile I drank. At seven miles a blister broke on my toe. My rubbing shoe made it worse until mile eight, when I forgot about a simple blister because both legs tightened. I forgot them when my tongue grew cotton, my side ache returned, and blood leaked out of a ventilation hole in my right Nike.

Mile nine, I died. I kept on putting one foot ahead of the other. I aimed myself where Rinehart suggested. I followed his instructions. He didn't know he trailed a corpse.

"Don't clench your fists. Don't hunch your shoulders. You're losing form. Drop your arms to your sides and shake your wrists. That relieves tiring mus-

141

cles. A change of pace will use different muscle groups. Sprint out."

My dead brain cells told me, "Run faster."

Run ten miles and listen to Rinehart's encouragement: "Looking good. You're riding your legs. Moving smoothly, economically. Eight more blocks. Two are downhill. See the finish line in your head. Think about it. Smile at the cars. You're looking better."

"I'm pretending," I gasped in my death rattle.

"Pretending to be fresh is the best psych-out in racing. Passing an opponent, you should act like you're hardly even breathing. You clip along, arms swinging low. High arms—he'll know you're tired. You want your body relaxed to fool guys into thinking they might as well give up."

I disguised my cadaver. I faked smiles. I chewed my Mungdrop energetically. I surged the final thirty yards in eighteen strides. My Nikes slapped our driveway, leaving one red footprint. Ten miles! "If this is what you plan for August, let's skip directly to September," I grouched. I emptied a shoe full of gunk.

Rinehart treated my foot with sprays and Band-Aids. "From now on, wear socks," he advised. "Two pairs. Cotton under wool. Your Nikes have stretched. Socks keep shoes from rubbing." He bandaged another bump. "This tape becomes wrinkled—I'll change it. Wrinkles here or in socks cause calluses."

Heat rash. Cramps. Unquenchable thirst. The pain. "You. Should. Have. Told. Me."

"September will be harder. Fair warning. Want to give up?"

142

I didn't. But why didn't I? Here I lay in my usual rigor mortis, dreading this afternoon's sprints, dreading tomorrow through November 3, day of the race.

Yet I'm getting conditioned. I hardly noticed the first five miles. No, I felt them. They felt good. My body wanted to move. I wasn't telling it to. Rinehart didn't coach a word. I seemed to float. For fun. If I could run five miles for fun, why not ten? If I could run 220's in 26 seconds, why not in 25?

I wouldn't have a chance to find out. That afternoon Rinehart switched me to 330's, rest, sprint 330 yards, rest, sprint. Lee High School never felt so unfriendly. Those extra 110 yards to the stopwatch blitzed my lungs. The track's surface punished my feet. Cinders had worn away in lane one. Ruts cut down my speed. And before that we'd had to climb barbed wire. My own school locked me out.

Rinehart knew why. "The football field's been replanted. Tomorrow I'll pick the lock with my autopsy instruments. I'll add them to my kit."

"You may need them for another reason," I said from my grave of grass seed. I'd finished running the stadium steps in ankle weights. I'd sprinted a few 440's for good measure.

Sprinted to develop a "devastating kick," as Rinehart described it. I'd be using a kick at the end of my race. Not a real kick, the kind Eugene shatters water coolers with. His footwork satisfies his temper. Mine would help win the championship. A kick is the fastest sprint, the tactic you save for a rush to the finish line. Rinehart figured I'd need to kick maybe a quarter mile out of the three miles' total course distance.

He'd read that the final quarter might have to be kicked in around sixty seconds. He named my kick *Zanbooming*.

August, I kicked 440's. One lap around the track at top speed was all I had to run—ten times per evening. 440 yards. Rest. 440 yards. Rest by walking 440. Kick 440 in 66.5 seconds. Rest and psych up for the fourth lap. I urged myself faster, stronger, harder. I kicked another 440 in 66.8. Another in 67.0. I psyched up faster, stronger, harder—440 at 67.1. Psyching up wasn't paying off—440 at 69.1. I told myself, "Kick better." How? Anyway, why did I want to do better in ninety degrees of heavy air on a pitted, lonely race track after running ten miles in the morning?

Rinehart called from his post at the starting line. "You're coasting both curves. You're tending to slow slightly before you reach the string. Think 'Faster' as you enter a turn. Kick *through* the string, not *to* it."

Now 440 at 66.1. 65.8. 65.2. Quit.

Quit and warm down by trudging the grass sprouts with my coach. He carried his thickening log. I said, "Why?" at the same moment he asked me. "Nothing else to play this summer. No one else to play with," I answered so he'd explain his latest theory.

"You run hoping to win that championship trophy. Two feet tall, sterling silver with your name on it."

"I never heard of a dopey trophy. I run because you make me."

"Aha. Easy enough to test. I'll be leaving on our family vacation soon. If you continue your schedule

those two weeks I'm in Maine I'll erase this motive."
He wrote: "Coach Rinehart."

First I lose my teammates and official Robert E.
Lee coach. Next I give up my favorite sport for one
I haven't even seen except in paper dolls. Now my
summer coach abandons me. Misery.

The night before Rinehart went away we took a
romp at Potomac Golf and Country Club. He had
read that many cross-country races happen on golf
courses.

"In the dark?"

"No, but when else could we come here without
being chased by golfers? I want you to experience
the problems of running miles on grass. Moonlight's
enough. Watch the ground ten feet in front of you.
We'll meet at Pollard Street fence."

We met a lot before that. I ran from putting green
to putting green, tagging the flags and staying down
the middle of fairways. Rinehart found shortcuts. He
popped up in unexpected places. He cheered me on
from behind trees and, naturally, gave advice. "Be
careful where you plant your foot. Don't step in go-
pher holes." He caught me beside a sand trap. "Run
through. Heavy footing builds muscles." He hid in a
clump of bushes beside a creek and convinced me to
walk through the water a dozen times. "Figure
where the footing is solid in a creek bed. Run at the
best angle. Other runners will splash and hope. You'll
attack water hazards intelligently, gaining seconds
on this."

He looped the loop with his stopwatch on its lan-
yard.

"And another tactic," Rinehart explained on the seventeenth tee. "Whenever you're out of your opponent's sight, increase your speed. If you're behind, you can close the gap by surprise. If you're ahead, you widen the gap without being detected. Zanboom on these right angles coming up. Then climb Suicide Hill half speed."

Rinehart hadn't brought his log. No reason to tell him why I ignored his coaching and kicked the highest hill in Arlington County. I used to sleigh down Suicide every winter, before the country-club fence sealed me out. I knew the hill's tough parts. I'd beaten this hill down. I'd beat it up.

Long. Steep. Brushy. Bouldery. I didn't lean into the hill. I strode erect, seeing my kid self trudging up pulling a sled. Back then I couldn't have run this killer for a ten-foot trophy of emeralds. Now I've mastered it for fun. I smiled on top.

Smiled into the headlights of a Jeep. Captain Fritz Slappy almost knocked down his teammate. "Whatcha doing around here?" he yelled from his driver's seat.

"Conditioning for fall sports." Not really a lie. Rinehart schemed we'd stay mum about my running career. Otherwise he couldn't be sure I wasn't training to read my name in the *Herald* as a hot cross-country prospect.

"I'm guarding this place. Whyncha go somewheres else? Wanna ride to the fence?"

"I'll race you." I plunged through the trees where his Jeep couldn't follow. I'd depend on tactics against a faster opponent. I saw Rinehart under Pollard

Street light. With a glance over my shoulder, I broke toward him. No Jeeps in any direction. Fritz knew he'd win, so he didn't bother.

"Fritz Slappy or any other big catcher couldn't outrun you long-distance," Rinehart promised as I explained why I wanted enemies. I felt I'd try harder with someone pushing me. "I'm pushing," Rinehart said about coaching.

"Not until you come home Labor Day."

"You're pushing with this." He crowned my head with his stopwatch.

The morning Rinehart left for Maine he dropped me off a pile of racing books and an empty log. He suggested I keep account of my training in an orderly, scientific way. I'm supposed to enter my miles per day, my running courses, my speeds. And, if I happen to decide at long last, *why* I run those miles on those courses at those speeds.

See ya, Coach. Write me your theories on a vacation postcard.

Chapter 17

First Day of Rinehart's Trip

I fell back to sleep after Coach brought me this log. Despair.

> **Total miles run today: 0**

Second Day

Woke up expecting slaps on my window. Bed until lunch. Misery. Does Nike Corp. make house slippers? What's a victory in the house?

Found out. Ran up and down basement steps. Kicked from living room to attic, 73 repeats. Best time, 16 seconds. Slippers slip.

> **Miles today: ?**

#3 Day

No mail from Rinehart, not so much as a forgery. I read in bed one book he lent me called *Guide to Cross-Country Racing.* It said: "Even if you finish last you've beaten everyone who didn't start." Including

Joe Donn! That sentence caused me to run my old course around the block in 5:20.6. I wasn't exactly backing up at that speed. Some truck tailgated me, but I outboomed it up the hill. It shifted gears, I shifted gears. My legs felt like Mung-oiled machines.

Miles today: 1

Entry #4

My hilly mile yesterday reminded me of an old question I asked Rinehart: How fast could I do the same distance on an official track? He never timed a whole mile at Lee High. Only intervals of 220, 330, 440, 660 yards. And mornings he's never pushed me to my limit. He's been letting me slow-poke 7-minute miles.

Here's my plan. Today I'll get back in shape by running ten miles to Falls Church at a 6-minute-per-mile pace. Plus a bunch of 440's, more than Rinehart calls for. Tomorrow early, I'll try for my fastest time.

Miles today: 13

Log Entry #5

Summer football practice at school! Fritz and Jumbo and them circled the field in a big herd of turtles. One look at Fritz panting—I knew he wouldn't be guarding anything later. I took off in another direction from Lee. I did eleven miles. Sweat but no sweat. Tonight I climbed the country-club fence to practice Suicide Hill. I ran roughshod over Fritz's golf course, up to my neck in obstacles. I love to vault fallen tree trunks. I love to sprint the scruffiest traps. I kicked the putting greens barefoot after my shoes drowned in the creek. I felt speedy. Rocks, knee-high grass—nothing slowed me down. I felt like a tree myself, so strong. I seemed to own Suicide Hill. I'm ready for my personal-record mile tomorrow.

Miles today: 14+

Log Entry #6, Sunday

Just when I'd forgotten about pain I learned more. I flunked my mile. I ran the first quarter in 61 seconds flat, my best time. I tried to hold that pace but slowed against my will. I went to the throttle. Every way I psyched myself failed. By the third quarter I staggered. The fourth lap I had no stagger, never mind kick. Shuffling the far turn, I gave up. I hung on a goalpost. I cried with a stomach cramp. Lucky the football team doesn't practice Sundays.

I learned more about myself. One of Rinehart's books says running's 90 percent mental, 10 percent physical. One says fifty-fifty. Either way, mental toughness and physical fitness aren't enough. In other chapters I read about the importance of pacing. Stupid pacing ruined me this morning. Pace is like an allowance. Say you get a dollar per week.

If you spend it all at once, you don't have a cent left for other days. Same with racing oxygen and energy. If you blow them all the first lap, they're gone the next three laps. After I read the pace parts I ran around the neighborhood an hour. I thought about pace. I seem to think clearer on the run.

> **Miles today: 1 hour, 6 minutes**

Monday Night

Pace means holding back.

> **Miles today: 15**

Tuesday, August 29

E.J.'s home from camp. She came over, but I'd gone on my morning workout. She came again. I'd left for intervals. She phoned while I captured Suicide Hill. I phoned. She's trying out for the volleyball varsity. She doesn't believe I'm not. That's because she's never scorched a pair of Nikes on a 14-mile morning, a 60-second quarter mile, and a smash through coarse turf. Fritz Slappy better guard Potomac GCC with a fire engine.

> **Miles today: 16**

Wednesday, August 30, night

I worked at my goal of a sub-5-minute mile before the track clogged up with snails in football pads. I felt a stitch in the second lap. I tried holding back but Buddy was watching. He showed up with the team equipment. I kicked until I almost fell down. Buddy said Monk got home from backpacking, but decided not to play football.

Miles today: 6

Friday, September 1, evening

Yesterday I received my annual picture postcard from Rinehart. Always before he's sent ferocious animals. This year he chose a person standing in front of a shiny monument. He wrote that my championship trophy would "seem as towering upon presentation." Further theories about me have crossed his mind: I run hills to feel dangerous; I run to get rid of excess aggression and energy. I gave his energy idea a whirl long-distance.

Miles yesterday: 17

A little while ago Monk drove past my house with his new license. He caught me kicking 220's on Military Road. I told him fall sports. I asked if he'd drive me into Washington on Labor Day. I read there's an official cross-country course in Rock Creek Park.

> **Miles today: 10 fast**

Saturday, September 2, 9:00 P.M.

1 mile at 4:54
4 miles at 5-minute pace
4 miles at 6-minute pace
All running at Lee track in a drizzle. Good practice in case rain happens at the championship.

Sunday, September 3, 9:01 P.M.

8 × 440's
4 × 880's
5 × Suicide Hill, different paths
1 hour slow-fast-sprint-kick, slow-fast-sprint-kick.
Changing gears important in cross-country.

Labor Day

Monk borrowed his dad's car for our trip to Rock Creek Park. Riding there, he explained why he wouldn't play football. Injuries have lowered his threshold of pain. And this strange reason—he loves to win too much. He said that after the Bristol play-offs he stayed burned up for weeks at the Generals who hadn't performed. Monk plans to learn an indi-

153

vidual sport, tennis probably, so he will blame only himself for losing.

Strollers and joggers crowded every path at the park. Monk waited in the woods for me to gallop one circuit of the 5-mile course. He didn't care if I wanted to run another. His mind still seemed to be hiking the Blue Ridge. My third time around I tried not to worry about Monk. I paid attention to racing. I noticed a wind at my back, helping me cross a field west. That meant it would blow against me recrossing east. I'd need to increase my pace to break even. Or—I could use a runner in front of me as a windshield. That worked. I'd discovered a tactic. Trailing the same guy, I found I couldn't see the ground ahead. That didn't cause trouble until we met mud. Not expecting it, I hadn't adjusted my stride. I lost seconds and inches. I passed the guy as we approached a narrow bridge. Caught behind him, I wouldn't have seen kids fishing along my path. I ran up through the trees around them. Now, in front of me, three joggers blocked my course. I had several choices. Keep behind them or go around them, again through trees. Both ways I wasted time. Push my way past—and maybe be pushed back. Or ask them for room to slip through. I called, "Honk, honk." They answered by giving ground.

My fourth circuit, Monk ran with me. We talked about his vacation. He'd carried a heavy backpack 500 miles. He felt in better condition than during any team sport season. I said, "Let's see." I picked up our pace in the thinning crowd. Monk stayed even. I poured on more speed. Monk had breath to ask why.

I struggled with myself to figure a theory. Why would I want to beat my second baseman? We streaked across the field, my brain outracing my Nikes. I'd be able to put Monk away for good on a hill. I'd hold the same pace until then. We flowed along together. We skimmed grass and leaves. We watched each other out of the sides of our eyes. "You look swell," Monk said when we slowed at the bridge. "You do, too." I meant Monk's tan. Under it he was falling apart. His neck and jaw were tight. The rest of him flailed or teetered or both. His St. Christopher medal flapped over one ear. I saw my chance to break him right there. I couldn't hold back. I kicked out of sight. Sprinting for Monk's car, I asked myself why. I stopped dead in the course. I waited.

Monk told me going home that he should've thrown me an elbow or squeezed me into the culvert our first mile. I silently wondered if I'd have squeezed back. Would I shove a teammate? He seemed mad I won. After a while he seemed not mad. But not happy. He asked what Rinehart had been feeding me from his lab. He suddenly realized I'd beaten him after running 19 miles already. He checked me over pretty carefully as I said good-bye.

Writing all this in my log makes me want to sort out the best parts of

20 miles today

I liked running an unknown course. I liked moving slow, watching trees stand still. Each step felt good,

155

not just the last step. It felt fine to swing along in the crowd. People waved. It felt better to pull out ahead. I loved it when Monk ran alongside me. That felt like old times. Talking to him on the run was fun. Plus matching our strides. Why had I separated us by Zan-booming?

Chapter 18

School began next day without me. I ran there in my fastest time. I said "Hi" to everybody. Ben Brown picked me up and tossed me to Jumbo. To them I seemed lighter. To Lurleen I looked better. Eugene saw me thinner. E.J. noticed I'd grown taller. Dum-Dum said, "Nope, shorter." Monk smiled. With friends I made the rounds of six classes. I had new teachers. I ate lunch with Rinehart while he read my log, schemed up my assignments, and forged me hall passes. I ditched last period, as usual.

But I'd never arrived at Robert E. Lee in my head. My mind and lungs and legs ran miles away. My feet belonged to my orange Nikes, and these were home drying from a drizzling morning workout. My heart rested, waiting to pump evening routes. My ears strained to hear track shoes slapping toward November 3.

September, I never showed up at Lee games. I didn't have time. Teams won and lost without me. E.J. captained her volleyballers to an undefeated month. Fritz quarterbacked a routine choke to the Redskins. All the footballers missed Randy Boyle's signal calling. Except Monk. He carried his tennis racket everywhere. He ran wind sprints with the Generals to improve his endurance on court. He was written up in the *Herald* for switching sports. On the

157

same page, a picture of Joe Donn Joiner glowered behind his football face mask. Joe Donn led the state in pass-option running.

Way down at the foot of football columns, in tiny print, Rinehart and I gathered news of the cross-country season. The same two runners as last year got all the ink, those paper dolls Rinehart cut out in June. I resurrected them from my dust-ball collection. Now they had names: C. C. Driggs of Bristol Consolidated; Palmer Stearns of Staunton Military Academy. Their eyes still hurt. I knew they'd hurt right through September if they'd trained as hard as I had. I'd stepped up my schedule to faster intervals with fewer rests in between. I'd done the school track early mornings when the Generals weren't watching. Afternoons I rode the bus around to different parks in Arlington and Washington, where I ran fewer miles but faster. Evenings I'd been lifting weights in Rinehart's lab. I'd learned from experience that my kick started with my arms—driving them harder along with my legs. Rinehart and I built a bench press. I pressed more pounds of iron every week.

Once in a while for a joke I pressed our logs, weightier than bar bells. Mine listed September's miles and whys. Rinehart's log recorded the cross-country season. Palmer and C.C. were definitely the runners to beat. They always won for their schools. According to the *Herald*, their tactics and times improved every week.

"So do mine." I lifted weights and talked to Rinehart. He measured out his secret formula I drank as a "diet supplement."

158

"Stearns and Driggs *race opponents faster.* You're *running courses alone faster.*"

"Alone counts."

"Hmmmm."

"Alone is fun, in case you never noticed. You can print that in *Rinehart's Human Newsletter.*"

"I'm measuring."

"Or if you just want results I'll enter a race tomorrow and try to whip those two. You'll publish a one-word theory: winning."

Rinehart fed me spoonfuls of protein supplement. I rested before skipping rope. He said, "Lee High doesn't sponsor cross-country runners. You know O'Hara wouldn't waste his players or his own time on minor sports. If there's no official Lee runners—there's no schedules against other schools. You can't appear at a starting line if you're not scheduled."

"Including the Virginia State Championship line?"

"That's easier. Teams aren't competing. Only one runner represents each school. I've sent in your entry blank. I forged O'Hara's signature. Say he finds out by reading the last line in the sports page—he won't care as long as you win. And you will. Meanwhile, for seasoning, you should race against other human bodies."

Together we chose Monk because Monk wouldn't reveal our secret. He recruited Aileen because she's speedy over short distances, and cunning. We'd have to take a chance on her mouth. Rinehart reminded her that he'd stuffed the queen ballot box. He offered her Mistletoe Princess in exchange for silence.

Aileen didn't curl her hair for our October workouts. She sharpened her elbows and let me have them as I tried to pass left or right. She sharpened her tongue to psych me out. I practiced being deaf. I tried jabbing my elbow to hold her off in narrow turns. She swerved a lot to make me run into her. She slowed down and speeded up unpredictably. Twice we wrecked each other. "She's tricky in the same ways as C.C. Driggs," concluded Rinehart.

"My tactic will be to get out ahead of him and stay there," I said.

Monk bumped harder. He wanted to win. I couldn't shove back. I don't know why. One day he said, "Pretend I'm Joe Donn Joiner. Crowd me. Slaughter me. Whatever—to win."

"I can't pretend. I know Joe Donn won't be running."

Monk dropped those tactics. From him I learned that kindness is a psych-out. At the starting line Monk grinned and shook hands with me. When Rinehart called, "Go," Monk whispered, "After you." He waited for me to break forward. On the Rock Creek trails he shouted, "Excuse me," and I'd move right over. He passed out compliments when he passed me. He loved my orange shirt. He loved my matching shorts.

"Thanks. We dyed them for my championship uniform," I used up breath saying.

"Nice guys finish first, if you let them," Rinehart cautioned me. "Palmer Stearns depends on courtesy as much as on his finishing kick. Ignore opponents. Run *your* race."

160

Who could ignore Monk's wide smile? How to reject Aileen's whizzing challenge even though I guessed she couldn't hold her pace for a quarter mile? I'd catch her later at my own speed. Why wear myself out hanging on her heels? But I did. She sucked me into her strategy once too often.

"I think I'd better practice pace at the actual championship course," I told Rinehart.

"The site's been announced. We'll go there Saturday in person."

"Where?"

Rinehart used his own psychology on me. He wouldn't tell where until we peeled south in Monk's car. Then he blurted, "Capital City Park, Richmond."

I shivered. I'd seen that place out my ambulance window—anyway, the spinning tops of its trees. I'd felt its hills after I'd regained consciousness. I remembered the park's choppy road hurt my arm. Richmond meant pain to me. "I suppose you'll be confiding soon that Joe Donn's running. You read it in small print." I shivered again even though Rinehart had tucked me under blankets. Up front he consulted a map. Monk drove, saying, "A skilled athlete will enter for Richmond High School, you better believe it. They stress every sport. But no football team member would race. The Redskins play their last home game Friday night. Any runner would be too tired—"

Rinehart interrupted Monk. "Cross-country runners and football players are entirely different types, according to my studies. Few could adapt, psychologically or physically, to the other's sport." He continued to lecture us on team and individual sports, extroverts versus introverts, aggression, hostility, obsession, competence, self-confidence, conditioning, stamina, speed, body types, lung capacity—his completed summer project on sports motivation. Monk listened like crazy. He almost rammed the park entrance sign, driving to Rinehart's theories. I didn't butt in. I'd decided to wait until after the championship to figure a true final reason why I ran.

Capital's course had been marked for next week's race. I walked the three miles, watching closely for good footing. I helped Rinehart lug our equipment in a suitcase. We paused to snap photographs of obstacles. We drew a map step by step. We measured angles of curves. We measured a narrow space between hedges. We took off our shoes and splashed through a cold, shallow stream bed to find my solid footing. We pushed a bicycle-wheel gauge the entire distance for an accurate log of feet, yards, and miles. At the finish line Rinehart said, "Length is precisely three miles, ten yards, and seven inches." He wrapped me in his overcoat. I lent him my ear muffs.

Monk huddled in the car. He'd been reading my log. He'd made up my mind for me. "Zan, you do it to break the string ahead of all other runners—the entire purpose of racing."

I didn't agree. I didn't disagree. I helped Rinehart load our gear in the trunk. We needed free hands for our second walk-around. For a ways we silently followed the white chalky line that bordered our course. My pal picked rocks off the path. I plugged

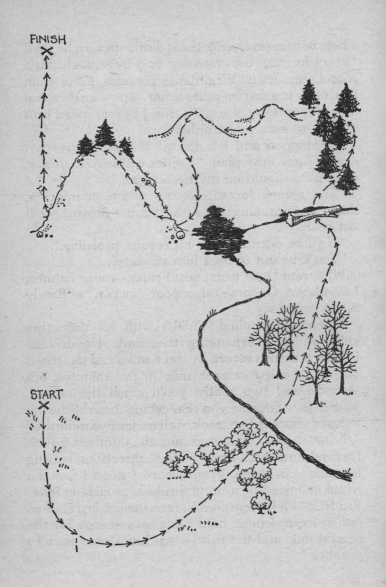

FINISH
X

START
X

a hole with moss from logs. At a smooth turn he said, "According to the *Herald,* only seventeen high school runners in Virginia do the mile faster than you. Only ten do two miles faster. Only two do three miles faster: Driggs and Stearns. But foot speed isn't enough to earn that trophy."

We stopped and I buttoned Rinehart's overcoat closer. I gave my plan. "Tactics will win. A steady, even pace should be my main tactic."

"The record for this course is fifteen minutes, thirty seconds, and six tenths. Palmer Stearns set it last year."

"He'll be out to better his record, probably."

"You'll be out to beat him absolutely."

Who would hurt worst next Friday—me or Palmer, I wondered. Or some other poor "sucker," as Randy Boyle would say.

Rinehart scratched 15:30.6 with his dissecting knife on an overhanging tree limb. He divided Palmer Stearns's record by three miles and scratched 5:10.2. "If you run each mile in five minutes, ten seconds, and two tenths you'll equal the record. Sounds slow because you're recalling those blistering miles of yours at Lee track, well under five minutes."

I drew a pair of lungs around the numbers 5:10.2. I waved Rinehart's knife in three directions, cutting the course in three. From where I stood I saw the white line winding among shrubs approaching Sure-Kill Hill. "I'll be tempted to race my flat first mile as fast as I can. I must hold back, save energy for the second mile and the third—that hill. Come on, let's practice."

We returned to the starting line. Rinehart's stop-watch clicked go. I leaped along the course. He would meet me at the one-mile mark by crossing the meadow in Monk's car. He would meet me again at the two-mile mark by short-cutting on foot through woods. At both points he'd call my times.

My legs remembered a pace from summer trips around the block. My lungs didn't heave. I ran slower than at Lee track. I held back. I psyched myself with "Save it" instead of "Faster." Save it is harder than faster, I learned again.

"Five minutes flat, too fast," Rinehart shouted at our first checkpoint.

The second mile I saved too much by tripping into a water hazard. "Meathead," I called myself.

"Ten minutes, fifty seconds," Rinehart blared. His math was right, my pace wrong.

Monk joined my third mile. He carried the stop-watch. He acted his part as an enemy. Then he played his real self, Mr. Nice Guy. I shoved both of him for practice. I sprinted with energy left from the second mile. In a few minutes he couldn't keep up. From the slope he timed my finish.

"Sixteen minutes," Rinehart warned, riding north to Arlington.

"That will place me about twentieth at the championship," I said.

We three worked on pace the week before my race. Those final mornings I went late to school with forged reasons. Those afternoons I left early to rehearse sand, mud, shale, and weeds that we'd drawn on my course map. Evenings I studied the map. Rine-

hart held it in place and counted my weight lifts.
Nights I tacked it where my shortstop glove used to
hang and studied longer. Before I turned out the bed
lamp I looked once more at my new team picture:
me, in drenched orange, after a three-mile run on
PGCC in 15:34.1.

I didn't say "CHAMP." I said "Ouch."

Chapter 19

MEET PROGRAM FOR THE VIRGINIA

CROSS-COUNTRY CHAMPIONSHIP

AT

CAPITAL CITY PARK, RICHMOND, VIRGINIA

Friday, November 3, 10:00 A.M.

Length of Course: 3 Miles

Course Record: 15:30.6

Course Record Set by Palmer Stearns,

Staunton Military Academy

(Program continued next page.)

Runners are invited to compete
in the Tri-State Marathon,
November 17 at Durham, North Carolina.

ENTRIES

No.	Name	School	Place	Time
05	Ashland, Tyler	Culpepper Regional High School		
07	Boken, Paul	St. Vincent's Preparatory School		
08	Brady, LeMar	Danville West High School		
11	Cronk, Harriman	Quantico Lutheran School		
14	Crowther, Bobby Gene	Portsmouth High School		
16	Dinwiddie, Cullen	Manual Arts High School		
17	Driggs, C. C.	Bristol Consolidated High School		
19	Fontaine, Wendy	Winchester Country Day School		
22	Greene, Jackson	Appomattox Technical School		
23	Hagen, Zan	Robert E. Lee Jr.-Sr. High School		
25	Hamilton, Matthew	The Priory School		
27	Hollins, G. Wesley	Baileys Cross Roads High School		
28	Hyde, Julie	Charlotte County High School		

(Entries continued on pages 3 and 4.)

Chapter 20

On page 4 of the championship program, final entry, I spotted 77, Yelverton, Dwayne, Richmond High School. I saw him in his red sweat suit slouched against the runners' check-in table, gabbing with guys in regular school clothes. He seemed more surprised to see me. I recognized Laddie Griffen, wearing a Redskin letter sweater. He pointed me out to Joe Donn Joiner. Joe Donn fierced his face and called out "Zanbunter," but for once he couldn't frighten me, not in his black cowboy boots, Levi's, and sheepskin jacket. He wasn't racing. He'd come to cheer his baseball pal, is all.

No one from Arlington had made the cold trip south except Rinehart and Monk. I expected that. We'd kept our secret so I wouldn't run for ordinary motives: Lee, bands, Mergler, pom-poms, O'Hara. All these other runners must be secrets, too, because hardly a person except them waited for the meet to start. Cross-country racing is definitely the most obscure sport going. My enemies stood alone, pinning flimsy numbers to the fronts of their shirts. Rinehart matched numbers against the program. He nodded at 17, Driggs, who looked fresher than his paper doll. Number 68, Stearns, wore white Tigers with his spotless white track suit. He never quit smiling. He joked with runners near him and slapped shoulders.

"Lonely business," said Monk. "Almost like tennis. You only have your opponents for company." He gazed around for a hot-dog seller. Monk'd skipped breakfast to drive me and Rinehart to our race.

I'd eaten my pre-race meal at Rinehart's lab, from a warmed-up dish on his Bunsen burner. It tasted like my old sling belts. So what? I felt full of energy without being heavy. Rinehart guessed there wouldn't be hot dogs or Pepsis. Anyway, those weren't good for me. I'd guessed there wouldn't be pro scouts. Or radio announcers. Or anyone but race officials in their red-white-and-blue hats. The few coaches attending took their runners aside for instruction. Mine had been given at breakfast.

The usual schemes. I should distribute pace evenly over the difficult course, but at one point I should try to break the others with a sudden surge. The Capital Park course favors experienced hill runners, so I should beware Julie Hyde. She trains in the Shenandoah Mountains. Driggs doesn't mean well. Avoid him physically. Don't be fooled by Stearns's psychological moves. Whoever runs for the Redskins can't be any good, don't worry, or his name would have turned up in the *Herald*.

"Like mine?" I'd asked.

"That's different. We shunned publicity in order to discover your subtle motives for running. Redskins thrive on newsprint."

Now I eyed Dwayne Yelverton dawdling toward the starting line. I said, "Rinehart, copy down in your log. I want to beat Dwayne because of—" I held up my right arm, my ex-boomer.

Rinehart wrote "revenge" on the same page as a pep talk he'd composed for the last minute.

This was the last minute.

Rinehart cleared his throat. "You have an extra advantage. These experienced kids never saw you run before. They don't know your strategy. If you're confident, you'll win," he read. "You've paid the price."

"I'm confident," said I. I'd swallowed his Mung for months. I'd swallowed his advice. I had a new arm, new muscles Rinehart built me. Bigger lungs, wider veins to carry oxygen around to every part of me quicker. Rinehart left nothing to chance. On our way to Richmond he'd used his dissecting knife to shave an ounce off my shoe soles. One ounce! Weight makes a difference, he knew. "Arthur, thanks to you, I'm confident," I said. "What else?"

He didn't read this part. He just closed his log and said, "Running long-distance is the most demanding sport. I've believed all along in precise numbers for your preparation: one hundred percent mental, one hundred percent physical; sub-four-thirty miles; ten seconds for the hundred-yard dash; fifty daily bench presses; five-foot six-inch strides; twenty-mile days; two-foot golden trophys; a one-thousand-mile total; one ounce—"

"Numbers count in sports," I agreed.

"You started with ninety feet on the base paths." Rinehart's voice began to falter. "Now...now..."

"Now I'm here at the championship starting line," I helped him.

"Alone." I'd never seen Rinehart look guilty before. He looked up at me and said "Alone" like he'd stuck me on a raft and shoved it out to sea. He said, "I've changed my mind lately about science. Just now—checking around at a real beginning—I'm not reading a book or a picture. Racing is about—" Rinehart thumped his heart.

Whatever he meant, I couldn't ask. A whistle blew. A voice shouted, "Runners, come to your marks." A hand holding the starter's pistol beckoned us. Along the starting line, runners spread four deep. Some of them squirmed and stared at their feet. Some tried to wiggle tension out of their hands. One guy went into a dramatic collapsing routine. Tall Number 25 snapped his fingers and pranced. A girl with shoulders out to here called, "Hey, LeMar, I heard you weren't racing today. You've been sick or something."

"Mono," Number 8 answered.

"Shin splints," somebody else said.

"It's too cold for my kind of race."

Alibis already! I couldn't think of one. The nippy air seemed perfect weather. My legs felt like ramrods. I couldn't come up with a psychological remark when Dwayne Yelverton brushed my right arm with his Virginia State Series ring. In front of me stood Number 16 with a skull and crossbones on his shirt. Next to him a girl wore one green sock and one red sock. I wondered why. Nearby a guy flipped down a pair of pilot's goggles. They made him look superfast. I hoped he noticed how winnerish I looked in orange.

Runners were impatient to start. Their chatter ceased. I closed my eyes. I put my mind on the three miles before me. I reviewed the course. I imagined the finish line. I took deep breaths. I relaxed every muscle. I opened my eyes in time to see Monk cross himself and Rinehart wave his ear muffs. Then Bang.

The getaway.

A crush of bodies left the line together. Caught behind them for one hundred yards, I had plenty of time to watch Yelverton shoving his way through. Within forty yards from the start, a Number 27 shoved back. Yelverton swayed. He leaned part weight against Driggs. Driggs pushed him off with full force. Yelverton tumbled, and few of us had warning to step around him. He caught shoes on every part of himself. Yelverton didn't get up after the crunch. I glanced back at him as I made the first curve. I saw Joe Donn, in his heavy, bouncing jacket, racing toward his flattened catcher.

So much for revenge. I'd have to keep running for another reason.

I charged headlong into the crowd. Wewereallascloseasthis. We sped together over the frosty grass. I heard steady breathing and felt a breeze from flapping shirts around me. Elbows tagged mine. Other hearts pounded beside mine for a change. I had running pals, tons of them. We're all in this together, I thought, except those loners—one, two, three—out in front. Stearns, looks like, in the lead. Then goggles in second and Number—

I lowered my eyes from the front-runners to my footing: frozen mud. And yellow shoes nearly stamping mine. The field we crossed was wide and flat. I schemed to weave through and burst out in fourth

173

place before we reached a row of hedges that would funnel us to the stream. But weaving takes more steps than straight ahead. More steps take more time, unless I upped my pace. I felt Rinehart's eyes on my back. He could still see me from his post at the starting line. I could almost hear his old cheerful voice saying, "Hold your steady pace! Hold your running form!" I'd better mind my coach while I'm still in his range.

"Dear Rinehart. I'm running your race," I thought.

Besides, I liked how it felt among flying hair and fingers and mud kicked back from swifter shoes. With these guys I was running somewhere for a reason, not just fence-hopping at midnight, charging up my kiddie sledding hill. We're all going the same way here on championship day. Our knee socks are slipping down together, our necks getting red as one another's. Numbers are flapping in every direction and number 14 falling off into weeds.

Julie Hyde called, "Beep Beep" to Driggs's shoulder, practically stuck in her chin.

Someone beside me said, "Oh, man, my ankle's gone!" and stopped with a jerk.

Directly in front of me two tall guys moved as a pair. Erect and loose, their form seemed perfect. They wasted no energy. Arms working gently, fists barely cupped—they made racing look easy. I hung behind them and admired their style until both broke away. They ran wide to their right. I watched them sail past runner after runner. They'd be hitting the hedges fifth or sixth at that pace. Oh, beautiful. Like Ben's swing and E.J.'s stretch from her bag.

174

I decided to follow those antelopes, to cut free from the pack with them. The pair made me feel graceful, me with my shorter stride and sweat trickling into my ears already. Plus I had catching up to do. Stearns was out there full of smiles if I could only get close enough to earn one. And the guy in goggles might want a second peek at my Nikes. After that, poof, I'd blow by him.

"You can do it," I told myself.

I sounded like Monk on the diamond. "Let it rip. Mow them down," he used to tell me. I knew he was back at the starting line with Rinehart. They'd be standing on tiptoes, straining to pick orange out of us runners about to disappear, single file, between hedges. When Monk and Rinehart lost sight of me they'd short-cut through woods to the finish line. I'd meet them there in eleven more minutes if I didn't goof. I'd hear Monk's victory whoop. I heard it now in my memory. What cheer!

"Dear Monk," I wrote him for thanks. "Don't be lonely in your new sport. I'll play doubles with you soon as I get through running. And we won't lose. Love, Zan."

Wonder if those antelopes write mental letters while they pass guys. They're in solid second place. Wonder if Julie Hyde means to pass Driggs right away. Driggs'll hold her off with a swerve. He's swerving. He's entering the hedge tunnel a yard ahead of her. Ten yards ahead of me.

Driggs increases his pace. Julie's no pushover. She has smart eyes, I remembered from the check-in table. Driggs better watch out. She's making her move around him, crossing the stream. Her long black hair swarms his face. She climbs the far bank in three strides. Her high backkick puts Driggs off his timing. He falters, calves deep in a pool he should've missed. I take my planned course through the sandy shallows and scramble up the bank where my mental map tells me to.

Leafless trees suddenly surround me. The white line I've been following is faint along here. It's been stomped into topsoil by front-runners. Never mind. I don't need directions. I know this course by heart. I'm two miles from Rinehart, Monk, the string, the trophy, the backseat of our car, where I can lie down for a while. This pace is faster than we'd planned. I can feel that. But I mustn't lose contact with the file of runners ahead.

Palmer Stearns.

Two antelopes.

The goggles.

A tan shirt with tiny print.

And Julie Hyde.

I count six. I struggle with myself to stay behind them. I must hold back while I still feel good. Later I'll open up when I'm drained. I'll gun down the procession, one by one. Right now, save it. Save. "Dear Aileen. You helped me learn pace. You taught me this tactic I'm ready to use on Driggs. You're my permanent Miss Virginia forever."

Driggs's breathing grows louder, raspier. He's riding my shoulder. His feet sound like dinosaur hoofs. His fists begin to skim my elbows, and I know I'm in for a nudge off the narrow path. I slow slightly to let him pull even. We run side by side, me gasping and choking loud as I can fake it. Driggs won't need to blow me away—I'm blown, he figures. Let him think worse. I'll fool him. Let him notice me dropping off his pace for the five yards that approach a fallen tree we must leap. I'm behind him, my eyes fixed on his nylon mesh shirt, same one his paper doll wears. I've seen it every night for months, and those baggy shorts I'm about to burst past, top of your jump. I turn on speed midair like a long jumper. I land beyond the frozen water hazard. Seven runners haven't broken that ice. Until Driggs does. I hear crackling, then moaning, then nothing because I've come to a clump of evergreens that muffles sound.

Now for my turn to be surprised! Off the course ahead is one of the antelopes. He's bent double, holding on to a bush. He sags more as I run near. "I went out too fast," he calls to my back. I feel what he feels: hammering chest; tightness behind my eyes; legs heavy enough to cave in the mossy path that begins to climb a short hill.

"Only a mile and a half more," I tell myself so I don't grab a shrub. Parts of me still feel fine. My arms, my—no, not them, but my teeth don't hurt. Running's fun, I convince myself once again. At least here downhill. "Dear Tammy Pam. You should do this sport instead of being a fan. You'd feel good and get piles of mail. xxxooo.

"P.S. This is not a forgery."

The chalk line curves left and points toward another slope. Bunched at the bottom are three runners—four. My vision's blurred by sweat, so I can't see who's beating who. I raise my shoulders and duck both eyes against my sleeves. While I'm at it I shake my hands and loosen my shoulders with one head roll. Wow. That Julie Hyde sure can step it. She's overtaken everyone but Stearns. He wastes time looking back. I'm rooting for her on this hill. After that I'm rooting for myself up Sure-Kill.

At the crest those one-two runners disappear, and not because my eyes are full of salt. They're going down; I'm chugging up at my planned pace. It's only my 5:10.2 mile, but fast enough to pull alongside the guy whose tan shirt says:

"If you're close enough to read this you're—"

Whatever I am, I'm gone. The last word stays behind me, and I'm gaining on Goggles. Right in here the ground feels comfortably runnable. Pine needles crunch. I smell them instead of the Mentholatum that Rinehart smeared where my shirt rubs my neck. I hear twigs snap. They keep my mind off my two-ton legs.

"One, two, three, four," I count snaps.

I'm on my toes, springing upward. I'm leaning slightly forward. My back is straight, not hunched or bent at the waist. My arms are pulling hard. My stride is quick—short—choppy. Smooth it out here on top. Smooth and pass Goggles, who's losing his form completely. Now boom downhill. My body straight. My foot-plant heel first. Lift knees, no matter how heavy. Relax. Relax, but don't skid on these leaves. They're thicker than last week, and drier. The antelope kicks them back on me but only for another yard. Suddenly we're a pair. I'm smooth as him. I'm erect, loose. I'm ahead.

Palmer Stearns leads Julie Hyde. Palmer—Julie—Palmer circling the ice-covered pond with Julie at his heels. I am third. Last week I ran first here and watched my lonely reflection in the water. Today I watch three shadows cast up Sure-Kill Hill to begin the final mile. Palmer. Julie. Me. We hop roots and dodge branches in the same rhythm. For two hundred yards we stick to a rough trail up. Then Palmer breaks left, maybe to find easier footing. Julie follows the course record holder. She must think Palmer knows a magic shortcut around the logs in our way.

Except for those logs I see daylight ahead, not Julie's swinging hair and Palmer's good-guy whites. I'll save steps by jumping. I'm used to this shale. I'm used to up and over whatever's in my path. I rush straight. I leap and drop, leap and drop only inches from Julie, who's back on the path behind Palmer. They've lost ground with their detour. Palmer turns his head to see how much.

His eyes say "Oh-oh," no mistake.

His mouth says nothing. What for? He's got a better psych-out than words. He works it on Julie. He lets her pull abreast. He blows her a kiss. Full speed up Sure-Kill, Palmer Stearns has energy to love his enemy.

Who knows what Julie's thinking? She fades so fast we nearly bump each other off. I manage to sidestep and spurt ahead of her. The pacesetter uses up breath laughing. I'm close enough to hear. I'm bearing down on him. I decide to kick and take Palmer before he hugs me to death.

Catch-up time.

But why? I'm in safe second place. There's a trophy for second and one for third place in case Julie revives and catches me from behind. Or some other runner zaps us. Fourth place, fifth place seem good enough for my legs. They're pleading with me to quit and coast to the string. I've already beaten everyone who didn't start—millions, zillions. I've beaten Yelverton.

I haven't beaten Rinehart's stopwatch. I'll race for the record. My name will be printed on next year's program. I'll do it for my coach. He deserves to see me pulling over Sure-Kill first. His telephoto lens is aimed at a pine grove marking the final half mile. His pen is uncapped to write the last sentence of *Rinehart's Human Newsletter*. Okay, here's your scientific ending, Arthur. I'm dashing past Palmer Stearns with energy saved for this move. I'm pretending to be fresh. Palmer can't know my chest throbs like the whole Redskin team's trouncing on it. Palmer's not fighting me off. No kisses. No smiles. He's had it. I feel worse. I've played with his paper doll so long we're old pals. Out ahead of him now, I can't think of what to do next. Say something nice, I decide.

"See ya," I say, like to my old Generals.

I'm alone, as usual. There's no one to follow. I've escaped my enemies and I'll soon see my trusty Arthur and Monk, once I'm on top of Sure-Kill. Boom. Boom. Boom. I stride the cycle of motion I've learned in Rinehart's outdoor lab: weight on one foot; float; weight on the other foot; float. I keep myself company by counting footfalls. I watch my two feet eat up ten feet between me and the pines. I reach to touch the first thick branch. I want to connect with something warm before I start my long descent to the cold silver trophy.

"That's taps."

My hand fumbles away from another warm hand. Then out from behind the pines races 77, Joe Donn Joiner, Redskin all over.

What does he mean, "That's taps"? What's Joe Donn doing here in Yelverton's number and sweat suit? And track shoes clomp-clomping beside mine? Can a guy substitute for his trampled-on teammate? Rinehart never explained such a cross-country rule.

My tired brain struggles to figure out Joe Donn's position. He couldn't be first. I would've seen him around the pond even with my eyes full of salt. How did he get here? I can't think. I can't remember passing a phone booth where Superman might change his Levi's. Presto, he's wedging his way between me and the trees. He's scary. I'm not so exhausted I can't feel afraid. I break my rhythm and drop back a fraction. Rinehart's lens will sight my worst enemy first, whatever Joe Donn's real position. Let him be first, who cares. There in front of me I can check what he's doing. He can't pounce. He won't twist my other arm.

But he will win.

On we run into camera range. Joe Donn follows the fresh whitewash line. He isn't fresh. His sweat flicks back on me. His face matches his scarlet jacket. I see when he turns his head. I meet his mean tired eyes. He must have charged hard on the shortcut that put him in my path.

I forget I'm running. I think about Joe Donn. His number's pinned cockeyed. He's rolling his head and thrashing one arm. The other arm is more like curled to hold a football. He's not using it for balance or speed. He's not Superman, either. Where's his cape? It would help him fly downhill better than those stumbly steps he's taking in Yelverton's shoes.

My enemy's slowing and our leafy path's widening. But I'm afraid to pass. Joe Donn'll whomp me in the chest. He'll muscle me into a gulch on our right. Anyway, why pass?

Just for the fun of it—the fun of being best. Best is best, that's what I decide.

"Dear Joe Donn. Move it. I'm coming past. Or through. Or over. I'll save you a piece of string after I get there first."

That string is only 400 yards away: three and a half times around the base paths, I tell myself. I push deeper. I hold nothing back. I bolt to Joe Donn's side. We go head on, elbows on, knees on, as we try to reach the same line at the same second. Every part of me booms ahead. My enemy answers by tromping on the heel of my shoe. One Nike shakes off on my backkick.

I spur myself harder. I blot out pain by convincing my lungs "Never again." I promise my legs a career's supply of rest if only they'll attack the final 100 yards in lengthened strides. I pull my arms higher and higher. I write myself a letter.

"Dear Zan. Run faster."

182

I do. I blow Joe Donn a kiss.

I mean it, too. I can love my enemy right around now. He's bringing out the best in me. I'm outkicking him. His legs won't catch mine over this leaf-strewn grass. One goddess of victory is all I need to enter the chute first. Of course the string doesn't break. It flutters away from my face and onto the finish judge.

Some other man tries to hand me a white piece of cardboard, but I'm slumped over coughing and swaying from Monk to Arthur. They hold me. They walk me slowly around the woods while the other racers join us one by one. After a while I can see the cardboard number that Rinehart holds for me: Number 1. Also I can talk. "Was Joe Donn second?"

"That creep. He ran illegally, just to harass you," Monk says.

Arthur says, "Joiner's little plot failed. He pushed you to a course record."

I feel too bushed to ask my time. I ask anyway.

"Fifteen minutes even."

I sit down to figure excuses for not running faster. I take back my promise to my legs. I plan other races. "Best is best." I explain to Arthur my latest theory. Before he copies it down, an official leads me away to the victory stand.

Three more steps up. Ouch. Turn around. Hold out my arms for the championship trophy. Heavy. I hand it to Arthur for our basement weight collection. I listen to the long announcement about us runners. I wait up here alone.